The Successful Consultant's Guide
To
Authoring, Publishing &
Lecturing

The Successful Consultant's Guide To Authoring, Publishing & Lecturing

by Hubert Bermont

Published by
BERMONT BOOKS

twenty-five dollars

PREVIOUS BOOKS BY THE AUTHOR

Psychoanalysis is a Great Big Help!, Stein & Day, 1963
Have You Read a Good Book Lately?, Stein & Day, 1964
Mine Son, The Samurai, Pocket Books, 1965
The Child, Pocket Books, 1965
The Mother, Simon & Schuster, 1968
All God's Children, Stein & Day, 1968
New Approaches to Financing Parks & Recreation,
    Acropolis Books, 1970
Jonathan Livingston Fliegle, Dell, 1973
Getting Published, Fleet Press, 1973, Harper & Row, 1974
How To Become A Successful Consultant In Your Own Field,
    Bermont Books, 1978
The Handbook Of Association Book Publishing,
    Bermont Books, 1978

ISBN 0-930686-03-9

© 1979 by

BERMONT BOOKS
815 15th St., N.W.
Washington, D.C. 20005

Printed in the United States of America

Table of Contents

	Page
Introduction	7

PART I The Consultant As Author

1. You Are A Writer	11
2. Writing An Article	15
3. Writing A Book	17
4. Finding A Publisher	21
5. Negotiating With A Publisher	25
6. Contracting With A Publisher	29
7. Proofing And Indexing	31
8. Scoring The Results	33

PART II The Consultant As Publisher

1. Your Own Imprint	39
2. Designing The Book	41
3. Copyright And ISBN	45
4. Book Production	47
5. How Many To Print	53
6. Pricing The Book	57
7. Advertising And Marketing Your Book	61
8. Order Fulfillment	71
9. A Different Score	75

10. Newsletters, Cassettes And Lists   77

Part III The Consultant As Lecturer

1. You Are A Speaker   83
2. Viability   85
3. Studying The Market   87
4. Chicken Or Egg?   89
5. The Ambience   93
6. Insurance   97
7. The Results   105
8. Forecast   109

Afterword   113
Index   115
List Of Clients   119

Introduction

LIKE YOU, I am a consultant. Like you, I am a successful consultant. *Unlike* you, however, I have been able to successfully broaden my income base and field of activity by writing, publishing and conducting seminars.

This sounds terribly arrogant on my part, I know. But, I was very careful, in titling this book the way I did, to select a particular readership. First, you are undoubtedly a *successful* consultant; this means that you empathize with arrogance and share a certain amount of it with me. Secondly, if you are already a successful author, publisher and lecturer, you wouldn't have purchased this book. Even if you succeeded in one of these endeavors in addition to your consultancy, you probably want to learn about the other two. To what extent and how I have been able to accomplish these goals for myself will be discussed in the main body of this book.

I am a book industry consultant; but don't let that put you off by thinking that I have an unfair advantage in writing and publishing. I shall offer my advice to you on your terms, in your language—whatever your field of expertise may be.

But, back to arrogance. It has its advantages and its drawbacks. My own particular brand of arrogance helped me considerably in starting my consultancy. I described this in detail in my book *How To Become A Successful Consultant In Your Own Field*. But this trait detoured and retarded my progress during my first few years by making me turn a deaf ear to other experts and consultants in other fields. Many of these fields interfaced with my own. To put it bluntly and shamefacedly, I got so used to *giving* advice that I couldn't *take* any. But, as I became successful as a consultant, I also became more secure as a *person*. At that point, I started to listen to my peers (I had always listened well to my clients). I do hope that you have reached the success and its attendant security which will allow you to listen *openly* to what I am about to painstakingly share with you. I know that:

   a) it will help you immeasurably in reaching your goals,
   b) it will give you concrete, step-by-step methods in reaching success in any or all of the three areas, and
   c) it will thus add one more success for me if you *do* succeed.

A candle loses none of its lighting power by lighting another. My sharing what I have learned with you cannot in any way hurt me; it can only help you.

This book is divided into three parts in their titular order: authoring, publishing and lecturing. Each part may be taken as a separate entity. But you will also find that they are very much interrelated. So read and/or study this book in whatever manner or method you choose and are most comfortable with.

H.B.

Part I.
The Consultant
As Author

1. You Are A Writer

IN MY OWN practice, I have many fledgling writers who come to me for advice about getting their works published. Fifty percent of these clients can't write at all and are summarily dismissed from my office. Of the remaining manuscripts, thirty percent have nothing important to say. The rest get my undivided attention. (All, however, pay my fees.)

You are in that special twenty percent. You are a successful consultant, *ergo* you must know how to write clearly, succinctly and well—otherwise your clients would never accept your initial proposals or your final reports.

I know also that you have some very special and exclusive wisdom to impart to others via the written word. Even though we are in different fields, you and I, we have an awful lot in common by dint of the fact that we are both professional consultants. Consultants practically never meet with each other to "talk shop" and swap stories. That's too bad. Perhaps we can make up for that here. Well, I've strayed a bit. Your wisdom, which I referred to, comes from the many, many clients who have come to you over the years with the same questions. After a while, I was almost embarrassed by the redundant, robot-like way that I answered these perennial questions. I would try to use different phraseology, different vocabulary, synonyms—*anything* to avert the overwhelming feeling that every time I answered I should have added "This has been a recorded announcement". But always the client was overawed and grateful. It continually struck me as most peculiar that none of them were ever able to pick up such simple, basic information elsewhere.

So I toyed with the idea of putting all of these basics into a book. A voice within me screamed, "Hold on there, stupid. You will be selling everything you know on that particular subject for six or seven dollars (on which you will receive a paltry sixty cents royalty) instead of selling it piece-meal, as you do now, for forty dollars an hour!" All too true, I thought. But then I pondered further. Certainly a book called *Getting Published* would give me more prestige, enhance my image and possibly get me more clients. It was worth a try. I teamed up with David St. John Thomas, Director of David & Charles, Ltd. of England. He was a friend, a client and a respected British publisher. The book was published in hardcover in 1973 by Fleet Press and by Harper & Row in paperback in 1974. The book accomplished all of the aforementioned goals and did not hinder my consultancy at all. To the contrary; I discovered that, despite the book's comprehensiveness, the reader still felt compelled to visit me with the question: "How do these principles apply to *my* project?" Such is the human ego.

So how does writing a book apply to your profession?

Whether you are a corporation tax consultant, a military electronics consultant, an advertising media consultant, a commercial real estate consultant, or any other kind of consultant, I shall continue to address you all in the second person singular to prove that the precepts set forth here apply to all kinds of consultants, and to illustrate how much we all have in common.

First, to repeat, I know that you can write clearly. Second, your clients' questions have become repetitive and fall into basic patterns. Third, your answers to these questions are, by now, pat, simple and to the point. Fourth, the fact that these clients are willing to pay your hourly fee for these answers means that there is no other direct referential source from which they can glean this information. Fifth, I know that you have the time to write about your field because, as a successful consultant, you know how to organize your time better than most. Sixth, being a successful consultant, you are highly self-motivated and far from lazy. These are all the qualities necessary for successful authorship.

Enough of this background blather. Let's get started.

2. Writing An Article

I SHALL ASSUME that you have never before been published. Rather than start with a complete book, write an article. Even though I had been published many times in book form before, I had never written a book as a consultant in my field. So I started with articles. Nobody commissioned them. Nobody offered to pay for them. I selected one concept in my field. It was a simple one, but a trap which seemed to ensnare most of the clients who were fledgling writers—vanity publishing. This is when an author pays a printer to print his books. The most obvious prey to vanity publishing is the military retiree, since he has lots of reminiscences, lots of time and a continued income. So I wrote a short, pithy, two-page article called "What Price Vanity?" and it was published in *The Retired Officer* magazine. Inquiries arrived and I gained a few clients as a result—but that wasn't the goal. The goal was the acquired discipline of putting my advice in this one narrow area on paper as clearly and as concisely as possible. Moreover, I saw my consultative advice in print for the first time. I then repeated this process several times regarding different subjects in my field. Later, there were honoraria; they ranged from $25 to $400. But these fees were both incidental and unimportant. I was sharpening my writing prowess for later. "Later" was the book, *Getting Published*.

Here are a few simple rules to help you get started with articles of your own:

1. Start with your basic premise.
2. Keep the subject narrow.
3. Write concisely and briefly.
4. Do not talk down to your audience.
5. Let your readers know how common this problem is.
6. Cite examples, being careful all the while not to breach your clients' confidences.
7. Tell your readers, in step-by-step fashion exactly how to solve this problem. *Don't hold back* on this information for fear that they are getting too much for nothing; you will definitely be rewarded for this later in some way.
8. Be certain that you retain the rights to incorporate these articles into a future book.

Your confidence as a writer will increase in direct proportion to the number of your articles which find their way into print. Remember, it is no slur on your professional consultative reputation if you are not paid for this kind of writing (the readers have no way of knowing this, anyhow).

Simple as that. Let's get into the "big time" now and move on up to the *book*.

3. Writing A Book

A NON-FICTION, "how-to" guide—which is undoubtedly what you will be writing (as I am writing here)—is nothing more than an article extended to book-length. Its organization and writing style are the same as those found in articles. Besides its greater length, the only other differences are that the book must have an introduction and an index.

You start by preparing a list of all the subjects in your field that you would like the book to cover. Then organize these subjects into chapters. Then list all the concepts you would like each chapter to contain. (At this juncture, I usually go through my client files to refresh my memory of cases in point.) Then simply treat each chapter as though it were a magazine article. As a successful consultant, you are probably so full of your subject matter that the book will practically start writing itself from this point on, i.e. the ideas will flow so thick and fast that your pen or typewriter will have difficulty keeping up with your mind. But you have to *start* the book to find this out; when someone just *thinks* about doing a book, the attendant feelings are usually helplessness and infertility.

A few words here about selecting a working title for your book. Let us assume that you are any of the types of consultant previously listed. I shall offer four possible titles for each which I consider to be poor, and then a fifth title which I consider to be good. In this way, the principles of creating a "selling" title will present themselves to you quite clearly.

A. The book by the corporation tax consultant:
1. *Seven Ways To Decrease Corporate Taxes*
2. *The Current Corporate Tax Dilemma*
3. *Corporate Taxes:* A New Approach
4. *The Corporation As Screwee*
5. *The Complete Corporate Tax-Saver*

B. The military electronics consultant:
1. *Seven Ways To Sell Electronics To The Military*
2. *Military Electronics Sales in The 70's and 80's*
3. *Military Electronics:* A Selling Guide
4. *Military Sales With A Very High Frequency*
5. *The Sales Handbook of Military Electronics*

C. The advertising media consultant:
1. *Seven Ways To Increase Your Media Effectiveness*
2. *Today's Media World*
3. *Media:* The Scientific Approach
4. *Mediantics*
5. *How To Choose The Right Media For Your Product*

D. The Commercial Real Estate Consultant:
1. *Seven Ways To Sell Commercial Real Estate*
2. *Commercial Real Estate Today*
3. *Real Estate:* New Approaches To Commercial Sales
4. *Time Now For A Commercial*
5. *The Complete Sales Guide To Commercial Real Estate*

Graphically portrayed this way, the "do's" and the "don'ts" become quite obvious. The five basic ingredients of a good title for a book like the one you are about to do are:

a) It must tell it all.
b) It should not require a sub-title.
c) It must be straightforward and not "cutesy".
d) It must reach out to the widest possible readership.
e) It must say that *this* book is *the* book on the subject.

So, *Seven Ways* to do anything couldn't possibly tell it all; there must be more ways. The words *"Current", "The 70's", "Today"* must be avoided at all costs because they put the book out of date in very short order. The third example in each case had a sub-title, which could have easily been transposed into the main title. The fourth example in each case was too "cutesy" for serious-minded readers, and in most cases unintelligible so that no reader or librarian would know what the book is about.

Here is why I carefully worded the fifth example in every instance. The first word *"The"* indicates uniqueness, or, the only book of its kind. The word *"Complete"* emphasizes the book's comprehensiveness. The word *"Handbook"* means that the book contains anything and everything that anyone would want to know about the subject at hand (and we know that only you can write such a book because of your unique expertise). Nothing describes a working guidebook better than the two small words *"How To"*. The selling ability of a non-fiction title cannot be overestimated.

By now you know that I am not one to tell you to do as I say and not as I do. I refer to this book constantly as an example of what I am talking about. I use the first person always and narrate my own personal history to exemplify whatever point I am trying to make. The main reason for this is that it is the *easiest* way to write. As Thoreau pointed out, the only person you can ever get to know accurately is yourself (for this reason he only read autobiographies, never biographies). You are most accurate when describing what happened to you; you are most lucid, and you are most interesting in this kind of narrative.

When you have finished your book, be certain that it is accurately typed (double-spaced) on white 8½" x 11" paper, and properly paginated. Do not index until later (see Chapter 7). Type up a table of contents for the front matter. Be certain that you have made a number of carbon or xeroxed copies. Your manuscript is now ready for publication.

4. Finding A Publisher

BOOK PUBLISHING today is enjoying most of its profits from the non-fictional, fact-filled, referential type of book. Accurate, hard information is what is selling today throughout the land. The "how-to" book on any level is the forerunner of the publishing industry. Along with that, the book that furnishes background material essential to accomplishing any task or project is enjoying vast distribution both here and abroad. The two vital ingredients of such books are comprehensiveness and accuracy. But a third and no less important element is credibility and accreditation. Your expertise, your client roster, your reputation in your profession or industry and your long list of accomplishments lend themselves immensely to your book's credibility as far as a publisher is concerned.

There are two kinds of books which will possibly emanate from a consultant's typewriter, i.e. it will either appeal to a wide market (examples: the book on effective media and the book on corporate taxes), or it will appeal only to a narrow market (examples: the book on military electronics sales and the book on commercial real estate). The wide-market book has more of a chance of being published by a commercial publisher than the narrow-market book, naturally. If the prospective readership of your book is extremely limited, you will have no choice but to publish it yourself (see Part II). The converse is not necessarily true, however; you may elect to publish the wide-market book yourself also.

There are approximately twelve hundred respectable book publishing houses in this country. (This does not include the "vanity" presses referred to earlier and whom you, too, should avoid.) Only twenty or thirty would be amenable to publishing a book in your area of expertise. The methods of singling out these prospective publishers are not difficult:

1. Any book publisher who has ever advertised in your trade or professional journals and magazines would be a likely candidate.

2. Any publisher whose titles are being reviewed in your trade or professional journals and magazines is another.

3. Other publishers who have produced titles in your field of interest would also be within your target area. Their names are on the title-cards in the public library index files.

4. *The Subject Guide To Book In Print* (published by R.R. Bowker & Co.) is another place to look.

5. The addresses, telephone numbers and relevant editors' names of any publishers you come up with may be found in an annual called **LMP** *(The Literary Marketplace)* also published by R.R. Bowker & Co.

A word here about a common case of paranoia. Publishers will neither steal your idea nor your manuscript. They are always willing to pay for the authorship of any books that they ultimately publish. However, if you have unremitting terror in this regard, the new Copyright Law permits you to copyright any *unpublished* work for a fee of ten dollars plus some paperwork (see Part II, Chapter 3).

Once you have selected the names of your prospective publishers, write covering letters to the appropriate editors. This letter should describe the theme of the book, its usefulness and your credentials. Do not telephone or attempt to visit the publisher in person at this juncture. Publishing people are most comfortable with the written word; that's why they are in that business. They consider phone calls and unsolicited attempts at visitation an annoyance and an intrusion. Notice that I said "editors" (plural). Your book should be multiply and simultaneously submitted to several houses—for these reasons:

1. Publishers are inundated with unsolicited manuscripts. They are all overworked and understaffed. (This is a business whose

net profits are considerably less than those of any other industry.) It may take some time before your book gets a fair reading—up to six months. If rejected, you have lost that time and must start all over again.

2. Although publishers abhor multiple simultaneous submissions and chant that they will take no part in what they call "bidding" situations, there is nothing unethical about it, they have no way of knowing that it is going on, and they have no way of controlling it.

3. If, by some good fortune, you receive contracts from more than one publisher for this work, you may simply select the better publisher (the more prestigious house or the one which can do best by your book) and/or the one which offers the best financial arrangement.

So make four xeroxed copies of your manuscript and send them all out at the same time with your individual covering letters. If you wish, you may just send an outline plus a couple of chapters; this makes it a two-phase operation, however, because, if they are interested, they will ask for the complete work, rather than send a contract. Be certain to always keep one copy of the work in your possession.

Do not in any way bind your work—three-ring, staple or otherwise. Simply put the pages in a box, preferably the one in which the paper originally came. Editors and readers get testy when they have to deal with fancy binders, clips or staples. Be certain that the work is properly paginated and collated and that any photographs, charts, graphs or line-drawings are properly identified.

If any or all four copies are returned, send them out immediately to other publishers.

A word about rejections. There is no such thing as an actual "rejection slip". Publishers are much too "gentlemanly" (which can sometimes mean "full of baloney"). If rejected, you will receive an individually written letter thanking you for thinking of their house and informing you that "although this is an excellent book and will probably prove very successful, it is not for our list at this time". Translated, this means that they think you have submitted an unmarketable turkey.

But time now to consider the opposite case, i.e. the positive. You have a much better chance in the publishing market than the average new author, because your credentials as a successful consultant bear tremendous weight on the authenticity of the book. So what happens if your manuscript is favorably considered?

5. Negotiating With A Publisher

IF A PUBLISHER is seriously interested in producing a work you have submitted, he will either express his intent in a positive letter, request a meeting or mail a contract—or all three.

Publishers, like all other businessmen, prefer to pay as little "upfront" money as possible for any project. No money is even more desirable for them. This money is called an "advance". It is an advance against future royalties. Let us assume that you receive a $1,000 advance on a book which ultimately sells 5,000 copies at $10 each and your royalty is 10%. Gross sales will be $50,000; your total royalty will be $5,000; your advance will be deducted and you will get a royalty check for $4,000.

Good publishers would prefer to use the advance money for either better graphics and production or for advertising—or for both. Short-sighted publishers would prefer to simply keep that money; advances are never refundable to the publisher should sales flop miserably. *Never* settle for no advance, no matter how eager you are to get published. Any advance at all—even $500—shows a necessary commitment on the part of the publisher and helps to guarantee your success in two ways:

1. It helps to guarantee the actual publication of the book. All contracts state that the publisher will publish "upon satisfactory completion of the manuscript". This means that possibly after

you have revised the book several times at his request, the publisher may still find the manuscript unacceptable. If he has paid you an advance, you may keep that money and seek another publisher. If no advance, you are out on a limb, having spent all that time and effort in vain. The higher the advance, the less likely the publisher can "pull" that on you. Or again, the editor who initially requested your manuscript is no longer employed there, and the new editor doesn't like the project. No advance leaves you no recourse.

2. The higher the advance, the more copies the publisher must print and sell to justify it. The more copies on hand, the greater the marketing effort he must expend.

The publisher gains ownership of the literary property, regardless of whose name the copyright is registered in. This means that he calls most of the shots. Rightly so, since it is his investment of money which will produce the book. The publisher decides how many books to print, how and where to advertise, when and with whom he makes deals regarding "residuals" and subsidiary rights (you will get 50% of this revenue), when and if to order a subsequent printing, when and if to issue a revised edition, and when and if to allow the book to die and go out of print.

Most important of all, the publisher's investment allows him to decide how much money to spend on graphics, art-work, paper and binding. All of this with the express purpose of *his* concluding what the market is and then *his* setting the ultimate retail price of the book. Incidentally, he also holds sway over the final title; recall what you submitted was a "working" title.

Now, you may have certain standards or ideas of your own regarding your book. If they deal with the design, appearance, price or marketing of the book, you must nevertheless allow the publisher to have his way and rely on his professionalism. However, let us suppose that the publisher, because of his cost-accounting, decides that he must eliminate a number of two-color illustrative graphs, but you know that they are vital to communicate the technical concepts you have put forth to professionals in your field, and that without them, the book loses a great deal of its use and efficacy. Here you must either hold fast or negotiate. If the publisher really believes that the additional production of these two-color graphs will price the book out of the market, then you might put up the money required and thereby subsidize the insertion of this second color for these graphs—or allow him to deduct it from your advance. So, too, with excessive photographs, four-color work, etc. But you cannot convince him to raise the retail price.

With regard to the technical and textual content of the book, however, the wise publisher and/or editor will constantly work with you and seek your advice and guidance. The more technical the book, the more control you will and should have. The more general the book, the less control.

6. Contracting With A Publisher

THERE IS A standard publisher/author contract; in the same way that there is a standard landlord/tenant lease. Most publishers pretty much conform to the same language, terms and clauses even though they may have individual characteristic variations. For the most part, the elements that these contracts all have in common are the following:

1. Names and addresses of the publishing house (known as the Publisher) and you (known as the Author). Tentative title (known as The Work).

2. Author grants exclusive rights to publish this particular Work.

3. Stipulation of royalties (in percentages) to be paid by the Publisher to the Author for book sales and the sale of all subsidiary rights.

4. The Author warrants that the Work is original and that he has sole rights to it.

5. Should the above warrant prove false, the Author agrees to indemnify the Publisher against any suit or claim.

6. An exclusivity clause regarding this Work and its subject matter. In other words, the Author may not submit another work on this subject to another publisher without the express consent of the Publisher.

7. All the Publisher's rights regarding sales and other disposition of the Work.

8. A schedule of proposed royalty statements from the Publisher to the Author. This is usually on a semi-annual basis.

9. A statement of any advances to be paid.

10. A clause concerning the Publisher's possible decision to allow the Work to go out of print. This is usually followed by the Author's rights to take possession of the page negatives (plates), to acquire the remaining inventory at a very low price, and to acquire the publishing rights if he so desires.

11. Agreement on the name to which copyright is to be assigned.

Be very careful about any matters outside of the above which you find in the contract. Also, if the publisher has a standard printed contract, pay particular attention to anything typed in.

Finally, a word about what the layman expects to find in a publishing contract, but doesn't. There is no mention about the number of copies that the publisher will instruct his printer to run. That is privileged information for the publisher, and since he is paying for it, he needn't divulge it. Secondly, there is no mention of the retail price of the book. That, too, is the publisher's decision and it is subject to change anywhere along the line of the publishing process—from contract time to publication date, and for a myriad of marketing and financial reasons. Also, due to constantly rising costs, subsequent printings of the same title may find the retail price higher. These decisions both belong to the publisher and are nobody's business but his.

7. Proofing And Indexing

AFTER YOU HAVE signed a contract and delivered an acceptable manuscript to the publisher, it will be copy-edited by him and set into type. You will then receive galley proofs for your corrections. Most often, a new author will think of many changes and different ways that he would like to say things upon viewing his material in print for the first time. This can be very costly for the publisher. As a result, he will heavily penalize you financially for this or simply refuse your changes (author's alterations). The reasons for this and the upset this causes in the production process are fully explained in Part II, Chapter 4. So try very hard to "stand pat" with what you originally wrote. Errors in typography are, of course, to be corrected by you and the galleys returned as quickly as possible. If there are many corrections, you will undoubtedly receive a second set of corrected galleys for your approval. Again, please refer to Part II, Chapter 4 for an in-depth discussion of the proper method of proof-reading.

Some time after that you will receive a set of page-proofs. This is different from the galleys in that your work is paginated in sequential order. It is now that you are able to index your book. The publisher expects this from you. In most instances, if you are unable to index, the publisher will hire a professional and charge you for the work. Or you may hire a professional indexer on your own. But indexing is not that complicated, and a quick explanation of it here could well save you $200 or more.

Starting at the beginning of the book, go through each page carefully and make a note of each key word, key phrase and concept (as well as all names). As you come to each one, record it on a 3" x 5" card. Throughout the process keep the cards in alphabetical order. Each time record the page number of the index word on the card. When you are through, go through the file for duplicates and record all the page numbers for the index word on one card in sequential order.

Then simply transpose all of this information in list form to 8½" x 11" typing paper, double-spaced. Send this off to the publisher, keeping the index cards for your own reference. Once again, you will receive this material in galley form for your proof-reading and corrections. That's all there is to it.

8. Scoring The Results

A S I SAID before, *Getting Published* made its debut in 1973 in hardcover. My co-author and I had received a $500 advance from Fleet Press, the publisher. (Coincidentally, most of my previously published books on diverse subjects were also done with co-authors, but this is not the norm. So let's assume that you will write yours alone.) The book was released at $6.95; the royalty was 10%. In 1974, Harper & Row bought the paperback rights from Fleet Press for an advance of $1,000 against future royalties of 6%; they issued it at $2.95. Since author and publisher split subsidiary rights monies, Mr. Thomas and I received another $500. Both editions are still in print at this writing, and in the interim, we have received approximately $500 additionally in royalties. So this book has earned about $1500 thus far. It will not earn too much more because other books have since been published on the same subject. Allowing for inflation, if this book were to be published today, it would command a $1,000 advance, the hardcover edition would retail at $8.95 and the paperback at $3.95. So the total earnings would probably not be in excess of $2500. Surprised?

Over the past fifteen years, I have had ten books published—all by reputable New York firms. Taken altogether, these books have earned no more than $20,000. All had "respectable" sales, as far as the publishers were concerned, i.e. they lost no money on these titles. Since writing was always one of my avocations, this was "found" money to me.

On the other hand, I earned $18,000 on two other books, but this was in my capacity as a consultant in my field. I "ghosted" a book called *New Approaches To Financing Parks And Recreation* as part of my retainer for my client, The National Recreation and Parks Association; and I wrote a book called *What a Waste* for my client The American Forest Institute. The first title was published, and the second one wasn't.

I did get considerable publicity as a result of *Getting Published*, however, and this helped my consultancy enormously. But the big bucks just weren't in it *vis-a-vis* the time spent on the writing effort. Generally speaking, you will have the same experience. There are exceptions, of course. Books like *Buying Country Property, Lasser's Tax Guide*, and *How To Avoid Probate* have earned combined millions for their authors. But you and I would be awfully lucky to have one of those.

No, your book will probably be somewhat akin to mine in that:

a) It will be written for a limited audience.

b) The publisher will not see fit to print more than 5,000 copies initially.

c) The accompanying advertising budget will also be limited.

d) Your earnings from it will rarely exceed $3500.

I am not advising you *not* to take this course of action. Actually, its a pretty good one when you add up all the benefits. And a large reputable publisher *can* do one thing for us that you and I cannot do for ourselves; he can give us wide and invaluable *exposure* via reviews, etc.

But if you want to do a book, if you have some capital to invest, if you want to make a *lot* of money as a result, and if you don't mind eschewing "image" and prestige, you will publish it yourself. This is what Part II is all about.

Part II.
The Consultant
As Publisher

1. Your Own Imprint

IN 1977, I wrote a book called *How To Become A Successful Consultant In Your Own Field*. It was inspired by the fact that at least one out of every two people I met seemed to envy my life and confessed that at one time or another they, too, had contemplated the idea (or the fantasy) of quitting the rat-race and becoming a consultant.

I utilized all the writing principles described in Book I—no more, no less. When finished, I felt that it was too good for those same New York publishers who had done so "respectably well" with my previous books. I sensed real money in this one, if handled right. One look at my partial list of clients at the end of this book will tell you that I have consulted with many companies and associations on the proper way to publish and market a book. So why not put my own expertise to work on behalf of my own book? I had some money, and proceeded. The story of this title will interweave with the principles of self-publishing which I offer to you here as part of this book, and for which I charge my clients, as you do for your expertise.

Armed with a selling title (see Part I, Chapter 3) and a worthy manuscript, I selected a name for my publishing company. For me this was simple. "Bermont Books" had already published referential sourcebooks for two of my association clients that had wanted me to publish for them. So I stayed with that imprint. I would advise you, however, to select a name for your imprint other than your own. A book written by John Jones and put out by the John Jones Publishing Company smacks too much of vanity publishing and has a negative impact on the public. The consumer would prefer to think that author and publisher are two separate entities. This is one strike against my books; you don't need any strikes against yours. So, if I were any of the previously exemplified consultants, I would choose imprints like the following:

1. For the corporation tax consultant,
   The Tax Press
2. For the military electronics consultant,
   Electronics Executive Aids Company
3. For the advertising media consultant,
   Pro-Media Books
4. For the commercial real estate consultant,
   Realty Press

Notice that all four imprints are wide enough in scope to allow additional titles by those consultants to come under their purview.

In all cases, it pays to have your attorney make a search to determine that your imprint does not duplicate an existing one; otherwise, you may start your enterprise as the defendant in a fat lawsuit.

You are now ready to design your book.

2. Designing The Book

ALMOST EVERY book you pick up, regardless of size or binding, has been designed by a professional book designer. If it is not, even your untrained eye can immediately discern the amateurishness of the way that it has been put together. The cover, whether jacketed or not, will be shoddy looking, the spine may be blank (making the book unrecognizable on a shelf), different type-faces on the title-page may fight with each other aesthetically, and the size of the typeface *vis-a-vis* the spacing (leading) between the lines may force you to read the main text haltingly.

There are, of course, all kinds of book designers with varying degrees of competency. But even the worst are acquainted with the basics described above as well as the proper placement of graphics on a page, the proper use of papers with different degrees of opacity, etc. Cut the cost of a designer from your book publishing budget, and you will be forever sorry and embarrassed. Unless you have been trained, you are incapable of designing a book—even though you may see the finished product in your mind's eye, know what size you want it to be, and know whether you want it hardbound or in soft cover. Furthermore, despite what his representative tells you in order to make a sale, the average printer is incapable of designing a book.

Book designers are comparatively few in number and exist mainly in very large cities. If you can't find one, work with your nearest competent graphics studio or artist. Most graphic artists are somewhat trained in book production. In any case, *this is not a do-it-yourself proposition.*

This is not to say that you will have no part in the design of your book. Your designer cannot work *in vacuo*. Different bindings, papers, sizes and colors are priced differently for one thing and give each book a different "feel" to the consumer, for another. This feel ultimately reflects whether or not a book is worth its cover price. So you must first establish how much you want to charge for your book before you have the designer go ahead. You cannot have a designer go his own way with paper, binding, color, etc., bringing the production cost of each book up to eight dollars, let us say, when you originally intended to sell the book for ten dollars. Conversely, you cannot allow him to design something which, when produced, will look like a three-dollar item when you have priced your book at twenty dollars.

Another reason that the designer needs your guidance is that there are decisions that only you can make because of your knowledge of your prospective readership. For example, this book which you are now reading has certain design elements which I, as publisher, deem necessary:

1. The typeface is very large and there is ample spacing between the lines, because my readership is you, the successful consultant, who must read facilely; your time is extremely valuable. Also, you are accustomed to reading typewritten material which is double-spaced (memos, reports, etc.) during most of your working day. The study and use of this book, therefore, must be *comfortable* for you.

2. The paper is exceedingly heavy and of high opacity. The weight is to insure the longevity of the book with the constant use it will probably sustain. The opacity is to insure that absolutely no type is perceived through the reverse side of the page. The book is priced high enough so that the extra postage which might accrue due to the weight of the paper will be absorbed comfortably by me.

3. The book is hardbound rather than paperbound because its textual material has a life expectancy of at least five years before revision; so durability is vital. It also travels better in the mails.

4. The colors were chosen for aesthetic reasons only.

How To Become A Successful Consultant In Your Own Field was a somewhat different design story, because I had a different readership. This was typewritten, rather than set in type (except for the chapter headings), because I wanted it to look like a personal report from me to the aspirant. The book was, indeed, extremely personal in scope. So I used offset paper (heavy weight) and an extremely heavy, expensive, vinyl binding. It came through looking like a quality report, rather than a book. I priced it at $20.

You, as I, must know how the book will ultimately be used; the designer does not. Notice that most of the above decisions were made with utility and durability in mind. Also, all decisions proved to be more costly than the norm; this is because of the money-back guarantee, which we will discuss later.

So, you must, in the first instance, convey to your designer your knowledge of your readership and your willingness, or lack of it, to add to the costs of your book.

Tell the designer your practical requirements, let him go to work, and be certain that he shows you samples of what he is doing as he goes along. That way there will be no misunderstanding and he will not produce a *fait accompli* which you may detest.

3. Copyright And ISBN

THERE ARE two requirements to certify a book. The first is the United States Copyright, which protects the work against any future infringement and registers it in the archives of the Library of Congress. The second is the International Standard Book Number (ISBN), which is an internationally recognized identification number for a published item.

Effective January 1978, the new basic copyright law now extends the copyright to cover the life of the author plus fifty years after his demise. You may now also copyright *before* publication.

To arrange for the copyright of your book, write to: The Register of Copyrights, Library of Congress, Washington, D.C. 20559. You will probably want to request a form TX. The TX application form was designed for "non-dramatic literary works". This is a broad category which includes "fiction, non-fiction, poetry, periodicals, textbooks, reference works, dictionaries, catalogs, advertising copy, and compilations of information". Accompanying your completed TX form, send two copies of the work to be registered as well as a $10 fee per title. All of this shoud insure proper processing.

Proper copyright identification in your book is composed of three elements:

1. The symbol ©, or the word "Copyright" written out.

2. The name of the owner of the copyright.
3. The first publication year.

To see a proper example, please turn to the copyright page of this book.

Take care that your notice of copyright follows the simple and succinct guidelines of the copyright office and is "affixed to the copies in such manner and location as to give reasonable notice of the claim of copyright". Time-honored practice calls for the copyright information to be printed on the reverse side of the title page. (Again, use this book as an example.) Most frequently, the lower third of the aforementioned page is utilized for this purpose.

The ISBN system originated as a computerized answer to the need to expedite processing and inventory control. Applying for an ISBN may seem, at first glance, a troublesome nuisance to you. However, if you entertain any hopes of eventually making distribution deals with other publishers both here and abroad (and why shouldn't you?), an ISBN is not an elective.

To obtain your ISBN, as well as further information concerning its uses, write: ISBN Agency, R.R. Bowker & Company, 1180 Avenue of the Americas, New York, N.Y. 10036. The ISBN is assigned to three places on the book. The first of these locations where this numerical code should appear is on the reverse of the title page with the copyright. If, for some reason, this is impossible, the base of the title page is acceptable. The second place is at the base of the spine. The third and final placement should be the back of the cover. If your book will have a dust-jacket, or special case of any nature, the ISBN should appear on the back of this as well. As a footnote, the ISBN must appear in type no smaller than 9 point. Legibility is vital if this number is to serve as an aid in the processing and handling of your book.

4. Book Production

MOST LAYMEN do not know that virtually no book publishers have their own printing facilities. Believe it or not! McGraw-Hill, Prentice-Hall, Random House, Harper & Row, *et al* give their book production work out, just as you will do. So there is no reason for you to feel inferior or intimidated. Furthermore, printing plants will send their representatives to your office just as fast for the opportunity to bid on your one book as they do to any major book publisher.

Conversely, no publisher worth his salt gives his entire list to one production house. Each book or series is treated individually; each gets its own set of estimates from three or more printers. So you are already "in the league" with your first manuscript and design specifications.

After design, there are basically four phases of book production:

1. Typesetting
2. Page mechanicals (paste-ups)
3. Printing
4. Binding

Since most printing houses have their own typesetting facilities (or sub-contract with an outside typesetter), paste-up people, presses and binderies (or again, sub-contract with outside binderies), it would appear to be most expeditious to have these four operations done by one house. After all, there is one estimate, one invoice, etc. It would also appear that you, the customer, would be able to maintain the most control and get the job done more quickly. Right? Wrong!

Cost-wise, time-wise and quality control-wise, you will do best by using a printing facility *only* for that which it is best equipped to do, i.e. putting ink on paper, and sometimes paperback binding. This, for the following reasons:

a) Printers regularly earn their normal mark-up on presswork. They tend to double the mark-up on the other processes. If their typesetting facilities are overworked at the time, they will sub-contract your job to another typesetter and add their normal mark-up to their bill. Also, most printers do not have facilities for binding a hardbound (casebound) book. Here again, they will sub-contract to a book bindery and add their normal mark-up. When asked why they add profit for work they haven't done, they will justifiably answer that they are assuming the *responsibility* for the binding and must protect themselves accordingly. But when you have made the decision to publish a book, you can shoulder these responsibilities, too, and save that money.

b) Typesetting firms, graphics firms which specialize in mechanicals, and binderies all make their living doing specialized jobs. They are usually better and more efficient at what they do than "general practitioners". They are also faster. It behooves them to get their work in and out as quickly as possible so that they can invoice and collect their monies. This speeds up the publishing process—provided that you don't hold it up on your end.

c) Handling these phases separately gives you better quality control over your book project. Each firm must submit its finalized portion of the work to you for approval before the book proceeds to the next phase.

There is one exception to all of the above. A large *book manufacturer* can produce the book less expensively than all of the above resources combined. These manufacturers are the plants which produce *The Valley Of The Dolls, The Memoirs Of Richard Nixon, The Encyclopedia Britannica* and thousands of other titles for large publishing houses every year. But you will probably avoid them because:

a) They are best geared for "long-run" productions, i.e. 10,000 copies or more.

b) You must reserve their press time months in advance, thereby possibly delaying your book. As a result, you cannot get a quick reprint order if your book goes well.

c) They are usually situated in small towns and rural areas. This causes delay in handling the checking procedures along the way and adds a hefty freight bill to your costs.

Whether you decide to use one printing house for all phases of production work or split it up as advised, you will find that the process breaks itself up into seven successive steps:

1. **Typesetting**
   Your designer instructs the typesetter concerning typeface style, size, margins and spacing. He does this by "marking up" the manuscript. A typesetting operation these days consists of one person sitting at the keyboard of what amounts to a computerized typewriter. (Hot lead type is virtually never used anymore.) This operator does not read or type for content. He or she merely copies word-for-word and letter-for-letter from the original manuscript. This is why it is so essential that the manuscript be accurate in the first place.

2. **Proofreading From Galleys**
   Galleys are now submitted to you for proofreading, and the original manuscript accompanies them for comparison. Everything we said about proofing your publisher's galleys in Part I, Chapter 7, applies here, too; but more so because this is *your* production money involved here, not some publisher's. There is only one completely accurate method of proofreading, but very few people use it (including professionals), because it requires *two* people. One person should sit with the original manuscript and the other person with the galleys. Then, by turns, to avoid sore throat or laryngitis, each should read aloud slowly to the other, including all punctualization, capitalization, etc. The person with the galleys will make corrections along the way, preferably in red ink so that they cannot be missed by the type-

setter. You can readily perceive the advantage of this method *versus* the normal one where one person has both galley and original before him, moving his head and eyes to and fro to compare phrase for phrase.

Symbols used to mark corrections should be clearly indicated so as to be easily understood by the typesetter. Here are the basic symbols which are both traditional and standard:

⌃ Insert comma

⌄ Insert apostrophe

⌄⌄ Insert quotation mark

=/ Insert hyphen

⸺/ Insert dash

⌃ Insert semicolon

⊙ Insert colon

⊙ Insert period

?/ Insert interrogation point

℘ Delete

℘̅ Delete and close up

stet Let it stand; restore words crossed out

∧ Insert marginal addition

¶ Paragraph

□ Indent

no ¶ Run in same paragraph

3. Reproofing The Corrected Galleys

Corrected galleys will be returned to you from the typesetter along with the original galleys with your correction notations on them. This process of reproofing does not require two people. You need only look to see that the errors have been rectified; the remainder of the text will be untouched. Both steps 2 and 3 should be performed with as much alacrity as possible and the galleys immediately returned to the typesetter so as not to delay the production process. You will be charged by the typesetter for corrections when they resulted from your errors in the original manuscript and when and if you made *changes* after seeing the material in print for the first time. Changes are costly, so try to avoid them; changing only one word can mean that its differing length from the original word could require the changing of several lines to conform to the design. Similarly, changing a phrase could necessitate the re-setting of an entire paragraph. Generally, you will not be charged for any errors made by the typesetter.

4. **Mechanicals**

The completed type now goes to the graphics people to be pasted up into page mechanicals. Just as the designer gave written instructions to the typesetter concerning the typeface and leading he desired, so too he gives detailed instructions to the paste-up artists regarding textual and illustrative page placement. The set of mechanicals is then completed, paginated and xeroxed.

5. **Indexing**

See Part I, Chapter 7.

6. **The "Blue-Lines"**

"Blue-Lines" (or Van Dykes) is the term for the only set of proofs that you will receive from the printer. They will contain the complete book, in sections (signatures), with the full text and illustrations. They should also be in proper sequential order. *Take your time here*! If there are any mistakes or changes to be made at this juncture, this is your last chance. You needn't proofread any of the text, because the printer hasn't touched it. What you are conscientiously looking for now are:

    a) errors in pagination

    b) misplacement of illustrations

    c) wrong illustration legends and page headings (running heads).

Be certain, too, that your designer inspects these blue-lines and okays them; this is his ultimate responsibility, and his eye is trained to catch errors. If there are serious and profuse errors, you may request a subsequent set of corrected blue-lines from the printer. Exercise this privilege. It will only delay the project by a few days, but "it's better to be safe than sorry".

7. **Printing and Binding**

The book is now completely out of your hands. So, for you, this is now "anxiety time". But, if you have meticulously done your part in the previous six steps, you will have nothing to worry about. The printer will either print and bind the books, or he will just print, fold, gather and trim the sheets and ship them on skids to the binder—who will, in turn, deliver the finished books to you. It is difficult to assay a time parameter for this process because of the varying degrees of size and intricacy of different books. Generally, however, if printed and bound in one house, the job should take 3-4 weeks; if done by two separate firms, it should take 4-6 weeks.

5. How Many To Print

BOTH THIS chapter and the following one must of necessity be placed in the wrong sections of this book—no matter where I choose to put them. Determining how many copies of a book to print and what to price the book are the two most crucial decisions any publisher has to make. Indeed, these are the marks of his professionalism, because getting only one of them right is not enough. A single wrong decision here can cause financial catastrophe.

The decisions are not made at this juncture. They are arrived at before the book is designed. But to have discussed these matters with you back there would have been confusing.

The answer to "how many should I print" is dependent, of course, upon how many you can sell. And the answer to "how many can I sell" is dependent upon the market and the retail price of the book. This may sound like a chicken-and-egg proposition, but it really isn't.

The cost structure of printing a book is no different from that of printing your stationery or calling-cards. The more you print on the first press-run, the less expensive the cost of each book, particularly since you have already invested so much in design and typesetting. But this is a trap! And this trap is the reason I have been summoned by countless clients, after the fact, to view untold thousands of books in living rooms, basements, warehouses, and even expensive office space with the same query: "How can I get rid of these?"

Although the price structure for a large press-run is enticing, you must bear in mind that a re-run at a future time will not double your costs, because the design, typesetting, mechanicals and page negatives (plates) need never be paid for again. So the short run is the best course. To be most safe, I tell my publisher and organizational clients to conservatively estimate how many books they think they can sell and then print one-third of that amount. But you are an individual, like I am, and we really don't have the foggiest idea of how many we can sell. Indeed, whenever any client, big or small, asks me to guestimate his future sales, I refuse to do it. To me, market surveys and all other such nonsense have no more efficacy than a crystal ball; and I refuse to be party to such merchandising inanities which are set up just to put the client (investor, customer) into a state of euphoria. So I recommend here that you do as I do. *My first printing is always 1,000 copies, no matter how optimistic I am*. I pay a penalty, yes, but let's look at the economics of this. If the design, typesetting and mechanicals cost you $2,000; if the advertising budget will be $5,000; if the printer charges $3 per copy to print and bind 1,000 copies and $2.50 per copy to print and bind 2,000 copies; if a reprint at a later time will cost $2.75 per copy (because page negatives are reusable); and if the book is priced by you at $20 per copy, then the sets of projected figures work out this way:

	Investment (Including advertising)	Receipts	Gross Profit
A. press-run of 1,000	$10,000	$20,000	$10,000
B. press-run of 2,000	$12,000	$40,000	$28,000
C. re-run 1,000	$ 2,750	$20,000	$17,250
D. total of A&C 2,000	$12,750	$40,000	$27,250
E. Difference between B&D	$ 750	——	$ 750

"Well," you say, "I'll invest $2,000 (investment B minus investment A) to make an additional $18,000 (gross profit B minus gross profit A) anytime." But wait. We are not dealing with investment, despite what I labelled the column; we are dealing with risk. Suppose you were wrong in the first instance about this book and its saleability. Suppose you wind up selling only 500 copies. If you had printed 1,000 copies, you would have broken even. If you printed 2,000 copies, you would have lost $2,000.

A word here about breaking even. In many ways, I am a very brash person. But in business, I am extremely conservative. With any new venture, I always look to break even at the outset, because breaking even in a new venture is being ahead, as far as I am concerned. Once the venture proves successful, or in the case of publishing once the book develops "wings of its own", then I am as delighted as anyone else to reap and enjoy the profits.

It is always best to be most conservative in this area of publishing. Even the large publishing houses have come to learn this hard lesson within the past ten years. They, too, are now opting for the short runs on all books which are not sure "blockbusters"—namely 98% of their lists. They now adhere to the principle: there is always tomorrow for the reprint. As a result, printing and binding technology has moved quickly to adjust to this situation, and short runs are now much less expensive than before; put another way, the penalty is not as great as it was before. This, of course, has proven to be a boon to the small publisher—in this case, you and me.

The "closer to the vest" that you play this game, the less your risks. I cannot repeat this too often. Another way to reduce risk is to bind only half of your printed sheets in order to wait and see if the book will sell. This adds a small penalty to the binding costs, to be sure, but it is less costly (if the book doesn't sell) than having a storeroom full of unsold books which are completely bound and paid for. In short, any way that you can "hedge your bet" in any phase of the book production procedure will ultimately pay healthy dividends. Remember that you are dealing with a narrow market and a limited subject. If you have misjudged your market, you have no other outlet through which to sell your books. Regular publishers can reduce the price the second time around, offer special deals to bookstores, or possibly even gear their advertising to a different market when they are in trouble. Most of these avenues don't always work, but at least they have options. You and I do not.

6. Pricing The Book

COMMERCIAL BOOK publishers generally use a rule-of-thumb by setting the retail price of a book at five to six times production costs. So, for example, if a book costs $3 for typesetting, mechanicals, paper, printing and binding, the retail price will usually land at $15-$18. The gross profit goes to pay for royalties, sales commissions, warehousing, invoicing, advertising, operating overhead, and the processing of returns (books unsold at bookstores are returned to the publishers for full credit).

But producers of *any* product in our system of free enterprise, who market by "slide-rule" on an invariable basis, are never in a class with the leaders of our business community who have flair and imagination. This latter group throws the slide-rule away. If a smart publisher has a book which is both unique and necessary, he will raise the price to the limit of what the traffic will bear. On the other hand, if he has a good book which must compete in the marketplace with other reputable titles on the same subject, he may lower the price to make this price factor the main reason for the consumer to react favorably. In other words, we have a situation of having an *exclusive* market *versus* capturing a *share* of the market.

As a neophyte publisher with limited marketing avenues and limited distribution channels, you cannot afford to compete for your share of market. Your book must be a first and an only. In other words, it must fill what we in the book business call "a hole on the shelf".

With a product like that you can charge a goodly price for your book. And you *must* charge a goodly price, as I will explain later.

Even though you do not have royalties or sales commissions to pay, even though you will not be dealing with bookstore returns because you will not be selling to bookstores, and even though it would be unfair to your book project to assign to it any of your existing rent, light, heat and other operating expenses, you will need a wide margin within which to work. For one thing, your advertising costs must needs be higher than that of a commercial publisher. By that I mean, higher per title. His new titles can be amortized by the fact that he already employs salesmen, he is already printing a catalogue with other titles, etc. You just have that one title which must bear the brunt of the entire advertising budget. There are three additional reasons for a decent price:

1. In spite of phoney market surveys, etc., you have no way of really knowing how many copies you will sell. If you sell less than your original print order, you will have a sufficient margin to break even.

2. You will have to use certain marketing techniques (explained in the next chapter) which will require the cooperation of other organizations and individuals for "a piece of the action". This "piece" must come from somewhere.

3. Although you will not be dealing with bookstores, you will have a certain amount of returns due to the fact that it will be mandatory for you to offer a money-back guarantee. The average for this return is 10% of your gross sales. More about that later, too.

Now I am not in any way suggesting that this retail price of your book "rip off" the general public. I am only trying to prevent you from naively thinking that, since you don't have all of the regular book publishing overhead, you can blithely *undersell* regular book publishers by pricing your book at two to three times production costs. First, your production costs will be higher than theirs due to your very small initial print run (that is, if you have taken my advice). Second, your advertising costs are higher. So, maintain the same general ratio as the regular publisher and minimally charge *five times* your production costs. Go higher if your book and your market warrant it.

Put another way, this is just one more method of eliminating risk. The commercial publisher spends 90% of his time trying to reduce that risk to zero; you must do the same.

7. Advertising And Marketing Your Book

I MENTIONED several times that you probably won't be selling your book through bookstores. Now I'll explain why. My reasons are based on experience; for ten years, I was executive director of branch stores for Brentano's, a large chain:

1. Your subject is probably narrow, and bookstores only take in books which have mass appeal.

2. Bookstores buy on a consignment basis, i.e. they only pay for what they sell. The rest they return to the publisher. This makes for an extremely poor cash-flow for you.

3. Even when they pay for what they sell, booksellers are notoriously slow bill-payers, and they buy at minimally 40% discount.

4. The books which they return to you are ofttimes so worn, dirty or damaged that they are unsaleable.

This indirect marketing approach being closed to you, we turn to the viable ones.

First let's discuss advertising. The two obvious forms are the print media and direct mail. You may choose one or both, but there are principles involved here which you should be aware of.

If your book is narrow in scope and appeals to an extremely limited audience, then the least expensive way of reaching your potential readers is by renting a good mailing list (from a reputable list broker) and sending out a mailer. The price of your book also bears on this, i.e. it should be substantial, because direct mail is the most expensive method of advertising per contact. When you see less expensive books advertised through the mails by large publishers, you will notice that almost always there is more than one title concerning the subject on the flyer. One inexpensive title is too risky for direct mail. A direct mail campaign, being as expensive as it is, requires as many risk reduction techniques as possible. Good mailing lists do not come cheap; they cost about $50 per thousand names (the range is actually $25 to $90 per thousand names.) So you are well advised to test these lists first. An excellent procedure is this:

1. Test six to ten lists with 3,000 names from each list. In most cases you will have to order minimally 5,000 names per list, but you can set aside the surplus 2,000 for a later time if the list pulls.

2. Be certain that the labels are coded by the list house; this only costs one dollar extra per thousand.

3. Be certain that your mailing piece is so designed that the coupon is back-to-back with the original mailing label, thereby "forcing" the customer to "tell" you which list he or she responded to (by the code numbers).

4. A 2½% return is decent. Anything over that is good. This means that your entire cost of promotion, book and fulfillment should be in line to yield some kind of profit with a 2½% return.

5. Some lists will pull well, some will break even, and some will "bomb". If only one list pulls well (hopefully), you will be ahead of the game, because you can now proceed with full confidence with a mailing to that "universe" (list), no matter how large and expensive.

6. Order more test lists and repeat the process.

Coupon ads are generally best, particularly when you find a periodical (magazine, journal, newsletter) which is highly respected by your readership. You will be astounded at first when you see the advertising rate card of the periodical in question, but don't be fazed. The higher the rate, the bigger and better the circulation—and you always get what you pay for. Be certain to always "key" your ads with a department number or letter added to your address on the coupon so that you can measure your results accurately. This applies to direct mail, too.

Another very important marketing/advertising approach is what we call P.I. or "per inquiry". Many periodicals will run your ad on a "space-available" basis at no cost to you. They split the gross receipts with you on a 50-50 basis. This is by far the least risky for you. Seek out the P.I. whenever you can. Newspapers, magazines and newsletters never reveal the fact that, on occasion, they run P.I. advertising. This is because they want as many advertisers as possible to pay their regular line rate. (A few actually do have a firm policy against P.I.'s.) So they must be approached carefully. For the obvious reason of increasing their profit share, they like expensive items in P.I. arrangements.

After some successful paid advertising and P.I. arrangements, I realized that, although the profit was much less, I preferred the P.I. ad because of the total lack of risk on my part. I commissioned my advertising copywriter (whom I shall further introduce below) to compose a letter for robotyping (each letter automatically typed but appearing totally personal and mailed first-class) in quest of P.I. ads. From *Standard Rate & Data* and *The Newsletter Yearbook Directory* I chose 137 periodicals whose readership seemed on the surface to be compatible with my book. This test cost $300. Bonanza! Within four days of mailing, I had five offers on the telephone. Within two weeks, I had concluded fourteen more arrangements. Indeed, the letter was so good (I never can understand the "why" of these things) that twenty-two of the people who didn't want the arrangement *wrote back* to apologize, to tell me why, or to offer to review the book free of charge. Thus armed, I allocated another $2,000 for this promotion, went back to my sourcebooks, selected 1200 more names, did another mailing, and reaped commensurate results. The best way I know to share this experience with you even further is to reproduce the promotional letter verbatim right here:

Mr. John Doe
Advertising Manager
THE EXECUTIVE REVIEW
Davis Publishing Company
1123 14th Street, Northwest
Washington, D.C. 20007

Dear Mr. Doe,

Electronic News (A Fairchild Publication) advertised our book on a P.I. basis and pulled over 600 $20 orders. As a result, the rest of the Fairchild Publications have been following suit (*Home Furnishings Daily, Metal Marketing, Energy User News*, etc.) with the same kind of returns. *Inflation Survival Letter* also agreed to a P.I. deal, and the publisher (Kephart Communications) made more money than if he had sold the same space at full rate! He is now running it in *Tax Angles*.

This amazingly successful mail-order ad is for a book I wrote and published: *How To Become A Successful Consultant In Your Own Field*. The tremendous appeal of such a book will be evident when you consider the number of salaried people who dream of being self-employed.

I'd like to offer you this camera-ready ad for P.I. insertion in *The Executive Review*. You may choose any of the three following arrangements:

1. Place your own name and address on the coupon. Run the ad, and forward the orders you receive to us.
2. Run the ad with the Bermont Books logo and address, obtaining a key or code from us in advance so that you will be properly credited with the sale.
3. If you prefer, prepare your own ad (or editorial write-up). Again, you may use your own address and forward the coupons, or the Bermont Books address with a proper code number so we know the source of the orders.

Whichever plan you select, *Bermont Books will pay you $10—50% of the book's retail price—for each order*. We handle the entire fulfillment operation: packing, shipping, postage, returns and refunds. All orders are processed on the day of receipt.

As each issue approaches publication date, you probably find yourself with some unsold ad space. Here is a perfect opportunity to fill that space and receive additional income—without expenses or risk of any kind.

How To Become A Successful Consultant In Your Own Field has sold 4100 copies in just five months—all through this one mail order ad. Yet the potential has barely been tapped. *The Executive Review* readers are ideal prospects for the book—as you'll see when the orders (and $20 checks) begin rolling in.

Got any questions? Call me collect at (202) 737-6437. I hope we'll be working—and prospering—together in the months ahead.

Cordially,

Hubert Bermont
Publisher

P.S. If you'd like a review copy of *How To Become A Successful Consultant In Your Own Field*, just let me know.

Back in the introduction of this book, I spoke about my new-found ability to seek advice from other consultants. It was at this juncture that this ability stood me in excellent stead. Another personal note here, if you don't mind. Many years ago, when Leonard Bernstein became famous, *Time* magazine did a cover story on him. They described him as the man most immersed in the stream of music, but not strong enough in any one area to alter the course of that stream. I have always likened myself to that description in the book publishing field. I can write, edit, publish, market, advertise, etc., etc., but I'm not the *best* in any one of those fields. Well, I had a chunk of my own money on the line here with this book of mine, and I wanted the best expertise. Two consultants were recommended to me. One specialized in his advertising knowledge of the media with regard to coupon book advertising. He read the book and gave me a list of media divided into two parts: the first part consisted of "musts" and the second part consisted of "well worth a try if the first part succeeds". He then recommended a crackerjack copy-writer to me who specialized in this kind of "response" advertising. This second man had a world of experience in his field and seemed to know every catch-phrase which has tested out to make people respond favorably to an ad like mine. You will learn what all this cost further on in this book.

On the next page is a reproduction of the advertisement in its actual size.

How to become a
SUCCESSFUL CONSULTANT
in your own field.

Have you ever wished you could quit your job and start working for yourself?

Well, maybe you can! Many people are amazed when they discover the tremendous amount of professional experience and specialized knowledge they've accumulated — experience and knowledge that others will gladly pay for. Literally thousands of people who made that discovery are now prospering as **independent consultants.**

The way to begin is by reading *How to Become a Successful Consultant in Your Own Field,* by Hubert Bermont.

Clear, straightforward, packed with solid information and advice, this authoritative manual tells you everything you need to know to establish your own independent consulting practice. Here's a sampling of the contents:

- What does it take to be a successful consultant? (See Chapter 1.)
- How to get started. (See Chapter 3.)
- How to operate your business — a collection of "tricks of the trade." (See Chapter 5.)
- What to charge your clients — plus five helpful rules on fees. (See Chapter 6.)
- Why you should **never** work on a contingency (speculative) basis. (See Chapter 7.)
- Ingenious ways to promote yourself — and make people want your services. (See Chapter 9.)
- Contracts: why you should **avoid** them at all costs. (See Chapter 10.)
- Just what do consultants do all day? (See Chapter 11.)
- How to market your ideas. (See Chapter 11.)
- Why you'll never have to worry about competition. (See Chapter 13.)
- And much more!

Perhaps no one is better qualified to have written this book than Hubert Bermont. He has served as consultant to more than 70 major corporations and trade associations, including the U.S. Chamber of Commerce, McGraw-Hill, the Electronic Industries Association, Evelyn Wood Reading Dynamics and the Smithsonian Institution. Yet he made the decision to become a consultant only after being fired from an executive position at the age of 43. You'll learn first-hand how he did it — and how **you** can do it, too!

How to Become a Successful Consultant in Your Own Field is just $20 (tax-deductible if you use it for business purposes), and you're fully protected by this **unconditional money-back guarantee:** Keep the book for three weeks. If you're dissatisfied with it for any reason whatever, simply return it and **every penny of your $20 will be promptly refunded** — no questions asked!

How many times have you told yourself that you're not getting anywhere — that it's time to think seriously about a major change in your career? **Don't put it off another day!** Clip and mail the coupon now!

Enclosed is my check or money order for $20. Rush me, postpaid, *How to Become a Successful Consultant in Your Own Field,* by Hubert Bermont. I understand that I have the right to return the book within three weeks for a complete refund if I'm in any way unhappy with it.

Name _____

Address _____

City _____ State _____ Zip _____

BERMONT BOOKS
Dept. WD, 815 Fifteenth St. N.W., Washington, D.C. 20005

In every case, these two gentlemen proved to be right. Here are some of the important things I learned:

I. Whenever possible, test your ad first. If it is a mailing, do a partial mailing first and see what the results are. If it is a newspaper or magazine ad, try one with what is called a "split edition", i.e. one that publishes regionally, so that you may test in only one section of the paper at a much lower cost. For example, I was told that the Southwest edition of *The Wall Street Journal* is demographically an excellent testing ground at a minimal cost ($660 for my 7" x 5" ad) and that a full-run in that paper would produce ten times the results of the Southwest edition. Sure enough, right on the button!

II. I was told that whenever a periodical had an optional surcharge for preferred space in the front section (first few pages), I should take it because the dividends in added readers and orders more than paid for it. Right on target again.

III. I was told that it was imperative to offer a complete money-back guarantee for any reason at all so that the prospective customer felt that he was taking no risk whatever in ordering my book. I was also apprised of the fact that if the book was decent and not a "hype", that return would rarely exceed ten percent of my gross sales. Of the first 1,000 books I sold, 50 were returned for refund. (My expensive vinyl binding proved itself valuable because it travelled well both ways and was returned in mint resaleable condition.)

IV. You will often see an advertisement for a book which says "Please add $1.50 for postage and handling". This is a bad practice because it irritates the consumer. It is always best to include postage and handling in the retail price of the book. The consumer has a very positive attitude toward the ad which says "Postpaid".

Enough. One successful consultant should not have to spend time convincing another successful consultant how worthwhile a good consultant is. Let's get back to marketing avenues.

Send review copies of your book (along with press releases) to every editor of every newspaper and magazine in your trade or profession.

If there is a book club which specializes in your field, contact them. Book clubs discount heavily to their members, so you must offer them a 60%-70% discount. But this would increase the exposure of your book and bring the cost of your copies down due to the larger print run, since they order in fairly large quantities.

You might be successful in selling a quantity of books to a foreign publisher in an English-speaking country. In other words, he would buy exclusive distribution rights to your book in his area. If not, you might possibly sell him the publishing rights for his country. A publisher in a non-English-speaking country could well buy the translation rights from you.

Professional meetings, conventions, trade fairs and seminars are another avenue of marketing. But with only one title, it will not pay you to attend and display your book, even though your potential readership may frequent these functions. The costs of air-fare, the display booth, hotel and meals are too prohibitive. However, there are several firms which are set up to exhibit for small enterprises such as yours. The fee is low: approximately $25-$50 per title. They are able to profit by exhibiting hundreds of titles. You need merely send them your check with a copy of your book after you have selected from their lists the meetings at which you would like your book to appear. One such firm with a good reputation is:

> The Combined Book Exhibit
> 12 Saw Mill Road
> Hawthorne, New York 10532

By now you really must be convinced of the importance of pricing your book high enough to accommodate the various marketing approaches which will eat into your gross profit. And what about discounts? Your association or a corporate client may wish to purchase much more than one copy—and they will expect a quantity discount. So a schedule like the following would not be remiss:

> 1 copy—regular price
> 3-5 copies—10% discount
> 6-10 copies—20% discount
> 50 or more copies—50% discount

Libraries request a discount, but don't always get one; if they need the book for their reference sections, they will order it anyway. A 20% library discount is more than adequate.

Additional marketing comes under the heading of what I like to call "pleasant surprises". These are nice things that come your way without any effort on your part. They are a result of "word-of-mouth" and "pass-along". Editors I never contacted heard or read of my book and requested permission to review it. Orders have come in as a result of these unsolicited reviews. People who give seminars have ordered quantities of my book to be used as texts in their courses. University libraries have ordered the book without any advertising on my part in their direction. And so on. This, of course, is the most pleasant part of all.

8. Order Fulfillment

ALL OF MY ads request payment with order, so it is rare that I must type up an invoice. However, if any reputable institution sends an order without payment, I bill them; individuals get no such courtesy. My procedure, therefore, is simple. A label is typed and affixed to the package. An accurate record is kept regarding which ad produced that order.

The simplest, safest and most expeditious way to package one or several books is in a book mailing bag or what is commonly called a "jiffy bag". You can save several pennies per order with other types of wrapping materials, but this is poor economy unless you are heavily into book publishing with a long list of titles. The space, time, and effort required for special wrapping will generally cost you more in the long run. Jiffy bags come in every conceivable size; the price is dependent upon the quantity, so order wisely. If you are shipping more than one volume in a bag, slip a piece of paper between the books so that the covers do not rub against each other and cause damage.

The United States Postal Service favors educational materials of all kinds by allowing a special, low postage rate for them. At this writing, first class mail requires 15¢ for the first ounce and 13¢ for each additional ounce. Books, however, only require 48¢ for the first *pound* and 18¢ for each additional *pound*. Since the average book with wrapping weighs 1½ to 2 pounds, you can readily see the savings involved. Along with first class rates, however, book mail rates are rising rapidly, so be certain to constantly check with your nearest postal authority to determine the current rate. To take advantage of these rates, have special shipping labels printed with your imprint name and address at the top, a blank space for the addressee in the middle, and the following legend at the bottom:

> BOOKS. Contents merchandise—Postmaster:
> This parcel may be opened for postal inspection if necessary.
> RETURN POSTAGE GUARANTEED.

Depending upon the postal zone, books generally take two to four times as long to arrive as does first class mail. Book customers are used to this, however, and you will rarely get a complaint unless the delay of the mails is untoward. This brings up the next point.

Be certain that any delay in book delivery is the fault of the mail system and not yours. The only way to assure this is by fulfilling your orders *on the same day that you receive them*! Considering the few steps necessary to get the books out, there is really no excuse for holding unfilled orders. "Our office was too busy" doesn't wash very well with disgruntled customers—especially prepaying customers whose checks you deposited immediately. *Do not* wait until the customer's check clears the bank before filling the order. Fill it the moment you get it. A delay of this sort is unnecessary and unfair because only two checks in one thousand will bounce. Awaiting check clearance is poor business practice in the mail order field.

If you fulfill quickly and efficiently, then there is only one sensible method of handling the very few non-delivery complaints which arrive after a reasonable period of four weeks or longer (allow still more time during the Christmas mailing season); *simply ship another book with no questions asked*. People are generally honest and do not try to get a second book free by falsely complaining that they didn't receive the first one. Non-delivery complaints are too infrequent for you to be hurt by this recommended procedure. On the other hand, if you are really *looking* for trouble, get involved with "we are tracing your order" or "we are checking your order". You can check and trace from now until doomsday and you will accomplish nothing except the waste of a lot of time. Meanwhile, your customer's fuse will keep getting shorter. Besides, there is no effective method of tracing a package through the mails if it has gone out book rate. Needless to say, a complaint should be checked first to determine that you received the order and payment in the first place. For this I keep an alphabetical file of every transaction on 3" x 5" cards. This file will prove profitable for other reasons, as you will learn later.

If, in the first instance, you are convinced that there is no way that you can include the simple procedures of book fulfillment with your other daily office duties, you may elect to use the services of a commercial book warehouse and fulfillment center. These centers exist in every major market area of the country. Some are more efficient than others. Check on three factors before engaging the services of a commercial book fulfillment center:

1. Contact a current client for a positive recommendation.
2. Be certain that part of the agreement calls for periodic inventory reports to you and total responsibility on the part of the center regarding any missing books.
3. Be sure that they will guarantee fulfillment within 48 hours after they receive the orders.

The fee for warehousing and fulfillment is generally 60¢ to $1.00 per order plus postage and wrapping material.

9. A Different Score

HOW TO BECOME A *Successful Consultant In Your Own Field* was published in March 1978. 1,000 copies were printed. One hundred copies were sent with news releases to various media editors, colleagues, and anyone else I thought would be in a position to help in its promotion; these, of course, were complimentary. I spent $5,000 for a series of space advertisements with coupons, primarily in *The Wall Street Journal* and the *Christian Science Monitor*, since these two newspapers tested out well for me. Additionally, I made P.I. arrangements with three trade newspapers and four newsletters. By May 31, 1978, my first printing was sold out. Having perceived the rate of sale by the end of April, I ordered a reprint of 2,000 additional copies; for this reason, I was never out of stock.

Fully confident now, I allocated $10,000 more to advertise the second printing. Continuing with the two previously successful media, I also ran ads in *Business Week, Retirement, National Review* and *Free Enterprise*. Some pulled better than others. The poor ones lost me very little money; the good ones made a very handsome profit. Meantime, pleased with their results, the P.I. media kept running my ads continually whenever they had the space. The actual numbers for these first two printings totalling 3,000 copies worked out this way:

Receipts

1200 copies on P.I. Basis ($10)	$12,000
1700 copies on regular basis ($20)	34,000
100 copies complimentary	—
Total	$46,000

Expenses

Postage 3,000 copies	$ 1,500
Jiffy Bags	330
Printing, first run	1,800
Printing, second run	2,000
Binding, first run	1,800
Binding, second run	3,400
Designer	250
Typist	300
Advertising Copywriter	350
Advertising Consultant	200
Advertising (space)	15,000
Advertising artwork	200
*Cost of returned books for refund	100
Total	$27,230
Net Profit	$18,770

*Only five percent of these books have been returned for refund. This expense item reflects postage and wrapping only, because all books returned were resold at full price. As stated before, the binding is responsible for the mint condition of these books.

(Note: the reason for the lack of differential or price break in the second binding is that the particular vinyl binding I used required mostly hand work.)

Two-thirds through the second printing, with no let-up in sales, I very confidently went back to press with an order for 5,000 more copies. At this writing, *How To Become A Successful Consultant In Your Own Field* is half-way through it's third printing, so I have no doubts about depleting it. Projecting these figures, I stand to clear $49,000 on this book project at the end of the first year. A totally different score, indeed. I wish the same for you.

10. Newsletters, Cassettes And Lists

SEVERAL YEARS after *Getting Published*, a tape cassette publisher contacted me and asked if I would be willing to let him produce a one-hour tape of my advice to neophyte writers. He offered no advance, but a 12% royalty on sales. I agreed, and willingly taped for one hour—my total investment. The cassette sells for $10. Royalties are just now starting slowly, but will undoubtedly increase. At any rate, it's all "found money" for me.

Probably I could enter this cassette tape business myself, but I prefer to stick to the market I know best—books. However, if your expertise assures you of a particular cassette market in your field, you may find this enterprise even more lucrative than books for these reasons:

1. Consumers are prepared to pay two and three times as much for a series of cassette tapes as for books.
2. Shipping and packaging costs are lower. Also, tapes are less fragile.
3. It is possible to run such a business on virtually no inventory. Orders can be filled by reproducing small quantities at a time from the master tape.

The primary drawback to this business, as I see it, is that the requirement of a cassette player limits the market. Large companies (like the one that produced my tape) offer players at deep discounts. I suppose I cannot see myself selling electronic equipment in order to sell one or two tapes that I might produce. It seems like the tail wagging the dog. So a royalty will do fine for me. At any rate, investigate either end of this industry for yourself after your book comes out. It is an additional bona fide source of income.

Next, I was made to understand by my direct mail consultant that the list of customers for *How To Become A Successful Consultant In Your Own Field* is worth at least $35-$50 per month per thousand names through a list manager. I was delighted to learn this and pleased as punch that I had meticulously recorded and filed all my book customer names and addresses. Before turning the list over to the manager, it was necessary to feed all the information from my file cards into a computer; to make the cost of this feasible, a minimum of 2,000 names had to be garnered. I completed all of these steps and expect to minimally net $5,000 from list rentals by the end of 1979.

Does all of this sound too good to be true? Wait; there's more. I was then advised from every direction, "Why not start a newsletter? You have an audience." Now the publication and economics of newsletters is a field within my purview and one about which I know a few things. I think it worthwhile to share some of this knowledge with you here; aside from everything else in this book, newsletter publishing might be just the thing for you in your particular area of consulting.

The recent tremendous growth of the newsletter publishing business is an accurate reflection not only of the publishing industry in particular, but of our overall economy in general. We live in an age of extreme specialization. Indeed, it is because of this that you and I are successful in our profession. Forty years ago, it was inconceivable for a merchant to make a living by opening a shop which sold slacks exclusively, for example. Today, a specialty shop can make it by selling only *denim* slacks. The general store is out; the specialty store is in.

Regional book publishing is now on the rise. Publishing firms are doing well just creating books about Vermont, let us say—or just putting out organic gardening books which deal with a small geographic area. It used to be the general cookbook. Now it's the Italian cookbook, the Jewish cookbook, the Oriental cookbook, and even the Vietnamese cookbook. The general magazine has fallen on hard times. So the moguls have switched to producing *Money, People, Body Building*, etc. Carry this to its logical extension with a massive, affluent, variegated population like ours, and we have the success of the specialized newsletter. There is even a newsletter on newsletter publishing! Because of the inexpensive, typewritten, short format, only several hundred subscribers can make this a very lucrative enterprise. Some of the annual subscription prices range up into the hundreds of dollars.

So if you are an expert in electronic sales to the military, let us say, your expertise doled out in dribs and drabs, along with hard news of your industry (which you get automatically by thoroughly reading your trade media) via a newsletter could be worth a fortune to you. Think about it seriously. If your information is "hot", you needn't worry about the price or your renewals. Your readership will pay well and stay with you.

As for me, I decided against publishing a newsletter of my own for an audience of consultants. First, in spite of my two books aimed at our profession, I do not consider myself a consultant's consultant (except in the area of publishing)—so I would not be the authority to write it. Second, there are already at least two consultant's newsletters that I have heard about; if I ever did start up a newsletter, it would be one that was exclusive. So I shall wait until such a subject within my field presents itself along with a viable readership. Third, at this time of my life, I really don't care for monthly or semi-monthly deadlines.

However, because my mailing list is so important (and still growing), I have had an offer from an expanding newsletter company who would like to capitalize on it in return for a royalty arrangement. I am pondering this now.

As you can see, the possibilities seem endless.

Part III.
The Consultant
As Lecturer

1. You Are A Speaker

THE SAME reasoning applies to your public speaking ability as did to your writing ability in Part I, Chapter 1. I have never come across a successful consultant who mumbled, stuttered, faltered or even spoke haltingly. Have you? The constant participation in important meetings, the oral reports and the training of clients' employees require that the consultant be well spoken.

Moreover, the best lecturers are those who only occasionally refer to brief notes and who speak in an extemporaneous fashion. The worst ones read a written speech verbatim, because they cannot think on their feet in an organized way. Again, as a successful consultant you have had much experience in organizing your thoughts on the spot, thinking on your feet, and fielding questions.

With this readiness, pick a subject in your field and offer a seminar. Executive seminars of every description in every field are now the rage of our business and professional society. As a result, these convocations are pouring lots of money into the coffers of the seminar leaders.

Does the suggestion "offer a seminar" sound like an oversimplification? Once again, let me explain in detail how I did it.

2. Viability

THE OPPORTUNITY here was really no different from that of the book. My national association clients all seemed to regard the publishing of a book as some kind of mystery, despite the fact that they had been successfully engaged in newsletter, magazine and journal publishing for years. Again, their questions and my answers in this regard became repetitious. So I sat down one day and organized the questions and answers. As with the book, a title presented itself. In this case it was "Book Publishing For Associations". If it were the other four exemplary cases, it could be:

"Cutting Your Corporate Taxes In Half"
"Techniques Of Electronics Sales To The Military"
"Doubling Your Sales Through Media Effectiveness"
"Inside Tips On Commercial Real Estate Selling"

My notes came to 120 pages of typewritten material. Figuring this to be 86 pages of typeset print, I published a manual called *The Handbook Of Association Book Publishing*. My research had proved that nothing like this had ever been done before. I priced the book at $30 and planned a marketing campaign for it. This was no problem for me, as you can understand.

But a seminar? How would I go about that? What should I charge? When and where should I hold it? What kind of advertising campaign was involved? How long should the seminar be? Was this an automatically viable venture just because no one had ever done it before? Would there be sufficient interest? Was there a market for it? I had too many questions and too few answers. So, I proceeded to figure out the answers as best I could.

3. Studying The Market

MY MARKET WAS the association executive—either the director or the person in charge of publications, or both. A bit of research seemed to point to the following:

1. My people liked "workshops" as part of their seminars.
2. They did not like to attend seminars on week-ends, because they wanted to learn only on the association's time (not theirs).
3. Although I estimated the worth of my two-day seminar to be at least $300 (based on ½ of my consulting fee per individual), association executives are used to paying approximately $200 for most seminars, no matter how exclusive the subject or how worthwhile the lectures. (I was wrong on this, as it turned out.)
4. They like at least one free lunch and several paid-for snacks during the breaks, thereby allowing them to enjoy some fellowship with each other.
5. They like to be given free study materials so that they may return to their organizations with something "tangible" to show for their trip away from the office; this also further justifies the seminar fee in the eyes of the comptrollers.
6. My seminar was one of many offered to the same people (albeit on different subjects). I had to be careful not to schedule mine in conflict with the others which had been planned (and even possibly booked) well in advance.

7. It is customary to allow a discount if more than one member of an organization attends. (I offered this, but no organization took advantage of it. Only one person was sent from each association, obviously with the intent of passing along the information when he or she returned home.)

8. To encourage quick response to the promotion, it's a good idea to offer a discount for early registration up to a certain date.

Most of these principles apply to most types of seminars and markets. Further detail from me on this, however, would prove irrelevant for different markets and different seminars.

I budgeted $5,000 for the entire project. (My financial situation makes me comfortable with risking this amount for most of my experiments.)

4. Chicken Or Egg?

THE SEMINAR was to take place in Washington, D.C. on October 16th and 17th, 1978. Always preferring to work and plan far in advance, I sought to reserve a meeting room the previous June at one of the finest hotels. I was shocked to learn that all the luxury hotels were completely booked for the next six months. It was necessary, therefore, to book into one of the best *motels*—a disappointment. I also believe that it eventually kept a lot of Washingtonians away.

At a meeting with the accommodations manager, I was asked how many would attend the seminar. This was a logical question so that they could reserve an appropriately sized room. Of course, at that early date, I had no idea. The direct mail campaign wasn't to *start* until after Labor Day; this was only June 20th! I could only take a wild guess (something which is anathema to me). "Fifty" I blurted. I figured twenty-five to be my break-even point, and arbitrarily added twenty-five more. "If I am terribly successful and get one hundred reservations by October 1st, could I take a bigger room at that time?" I inquired. Not on your life. These meeting rooms were as scarce as hens' teeth; hence the need to reserve so far in advance. And what if the campaign failed and it was necessary to cancel the room reservation altogether? Tough luck; I would be stuck with the rental fee for those two days whether I used the space or not. I would not, however, be stuck for the larger luncheon bill, because this could be cancelled one week before the scheduled seminar. Thank goodness.

I came away from that meeting with the feeling of a "high roller" at Las Vegas who had just bet $200 on one number of the roulette wheel.

This was indeed a "chicken or egg" proposition, and there was no way of intelligently planning anything before we had the necessary information. Being a logical, conservative person, I began to experience mounting anxiety.

While at that meeting, the accommodations manager read off a check-list which forced me to think about other matters which had not dawned on me up to that point, and which required decisions. In rapid-fire style, I was asked the following questions:

1. What price-range luncheon did I wish to order?
2. Within that price range, what menu did I want?
3. Did I wish to pay for drinks or have the management set up a cash bar?
4. Did I want coffee breaks? If so, how many?
5. Was the morning coffee break to be accompanied by Danish pastry?
6. Would I require any blackboards, easels and/or audio/visual equipment? (These were all available through the management on a rental-fee basis.)
7. Would I require any signs? (Fee basis.)
8. Would I require personnel for the registration prior to the seminar? (Fee basis.)
9. Would I require a public address system? (Fee basis.)
10. Would I require storage space for my materials the night before the seminar? (No charge for this; would you believe it?)
11. Would I like the seminar to be recorded and taped in cassette form? (Fee basis.)

My head swam. I decided to go back to my office and think these things over before answering. In effect, I was really being asked "What kind of a seminar would you like to run here?" A fitting question.

5. The Ambience

I HAVE PAID GOOD money to attend a number of seminars in my lifetime, as you probably have. Every one of them left me disgruntled. I never felt that any of them were topnotch, worth the price or taught me as much as I had expected from the advertising brochure. Looking back and analyzing them in June of 1978, I sought the reasons for what I considered to be their failures:

1. Either they served no lunch and allowed me to fend for myself in a strange place, thereby costing me needless time—or, they served such a sumptuous meal that I was groggy for the rest of the afternoon.

2. Many times, free booze was unlimited, and a goodly number of my fellow attendees were totally smashed. Sometimes, the seminar leader was, too.

3. They relied very heavily on audio/visuals of the most juvenile kind. The leader would make a simple, declarative statement like "Translation rights may be sold in any of three ways: directly to a foreign publisher, through a foreign agent or at an international book fair." Lo and behold, the lights would go out, and a slide would appear on a screen. On the slide was printed:

   I   FOREIGN PUBLISHER
   II FOREIGN AGENT
   III INTERNATIONAL BOOK FAIR

Sometimes this would be broken up into three separate slides; and often these slides would be illustrated with a cartoon. Thus the day went: lights off, lights on, lights off, lights on, etc. Additionally, the person operating the equipment appeared **to** be totally bored all day and was a distraction. Whenever **the** lights went back on, half the audience was asleep.

4. I never attended a seminar with a public address system where the leader was versed in the proper techniques and use of a microphone. Raucous noise, too much volume and electronic feedback were the order of the day.

Recalling all of these negative aspects of seminars, I made up my mind as to the kind of seminar I wanted to give. I remembered what Mark Twain used to tell his lecture audiences before each break: "It's a terrible death to be talked to death."

My first decision was based on a theatrical principle: Better to rent a smaller room and pack it than to rent a large room and possibly have it half filled.

My second decision was based on a television principle: Avoid overexposure. If great personalities wear out their welcome by showing themselves every week for one hour, I would probably be a disaster on my own for two straight days. So I planned the seminar as a panel show, enlisting the services of a printer, a bindery man and a graphics expert to share the podium with me. Panelists of this kind want the exposure and generally do not charge for their time.

I further decided against blackboards, easels or audio/visual aids of any kind. Instead, I prepared to set up a schoolroom situation with each attendee behind his own desk with his own manuals, specimens, exemplary books and equipment for taking notes.

I selected an elegant but light lunch, a cash bar and two coffee breaks each day.

To eliminate any depersonalizing effect, I eschewed a microphone and public address system. (My voice carries well.)

All other decisions were put off until the time when I could determine the general response to my promotional campaign.

In a sense, my concept of a seminar reflected who I am. Similarly, the seminar you give will be an extension of who you are.

6. Insurance

I HELD A MEETING at the end of June with my advertising copyrighter to plan the mailing piece. On several occasions during the meeting I expressed my extreme discomfiture and anxiety concerning what I called the "crapshoot" of risking all that money on one mailing. I would have been much more comfortable if we could have tested the mailing first. But there was no time for this since the distribution of the flyers would be immediately after Labor Day— five weeks before the seminar.

We finally came up with what I like to call *an insurance policy*. Why not, in a secondary fashion, promote the handbook I had published. We could infer that, if for some reason the prospect couldn't attend the seminar—distance, lack of time, conflict of time or the $225 fee—he could order the book for $30. The handbook was not quite the same in that it couldn't provide the hands-on workshop of the seminar, but it was the textbook for the seminar. In this way, if for any one of a hundred reasons the seminar proved to be a financial failure, sales of the books would partially make up for the loss. I felt an overwhelming sense of relief.

Nine chances out of ten, if you publish a book *and* run a seminar, they will both be on the same subject, i.e. your exclusive consultative specialty. So bear this "insurance policy" in mind. But it must be worded just right. You can't lead the prospect to believe that book and seminar are equally effective at such disparate prices; if you do, you will ruin the primary purpose of your seminar promotion. Conversely, you cannot allow the prospect to think that without the seminar the book is worthless, because that isn't true either.

I have taken pains to reproduce the text of my mailing piece so that you can see all the ingredients that a good copywriter includes and so that you can see how the dual promotion (seminar and book) was worded and where the emphasis was placed. (Unfortunately I am unable to reproduce the actual piece here graphically because of it's unusual shape and size.) The mailer was printed in two colors.

BOOK PUBLISHING FOR ASSOCIATIONS

A comprehensive two-day seminar: Monday and Tuesday, Oct. 16, & 17, 1978, Washington D.C.

Why a book publishing seminar for associations?

Today, more than ever before, professional and trade associations are becoming interested in publishing beyond the usual newsletter and journal. And with good reason: association-published books can increase an institution's visibility, its prestige, its non-dues revenue.

Yet the association executive very often feels intimidated by the prospect of getting a book written and published. He may have no experience in publishing (other than his association's periodical), and is therefore hesitant to venture into unfamiliar territory.

According to Hubert Bermont, such fears are unwarranted. A nationally-known book consultant, Mr. Bermont has been responsible for the publication of more than 75 association books.

"Don't be afraid of book publishing," Bermont tells association execs.

"There's no reason for an association to be scared away from book publishing," says Mr. Bermont. "There's no special mystique to this field. Dozens of associations with no previous publishing experience have turned out successful book projects. I know. I've helped them do it.

"But you *do* have to know a few basics. Book publishing is totally different from periodical publishing. It requires different skills, different resources, different knowledge."

The Seminar.

To acquaint association executives with these fundamental principles and techniques, Mr. Bermont has organized the first and only seminar on *Book Publishing for Associations*.

This intensive two-day seminar will teach the association executive what he needs to know to successfully publish his book. Everything is covered: writing, editing, printing, marketing, publicity, distribution. Stressed throughout the seminar are *the key principles of effective management* that will minimize risk and help ensure success.

Once the association has decided to publish a book, it faces another important choice: whether to contract with an established publishing house, or to publish the book itself. The seminar will cover both options: the first day will treat *the association as author*—and show how the association can act as its own literary agent. The second day will treat *the association as publisher* of its own books.

Throughout both days, there will be ample opportunity for you to consult personally with the seminar leaders. You're even invited to bring along your own book project for discussion and critique in a special "hands-on" publishing workshop.

The advantages of publishing.

Book publishing offers the association numerous benefits—benefits few associations are now realizing.

One of the association's most important functions is communication with its members. Yet the newsletter, journal or magazine is often limited in accomplishing this goal. A handbook, technical manual, "how-to" book, reference work or other book-length treatment is often warranted.

What's more, *such a book may have a vast market well beyond the association's immediate membership.* The Smithsonian Institution, the National Geographic Society and the Brookings Institution are among the organizations that have enormously successful book publishing operations and can boast numerous "best sellers." These and many other associations have realized an increase in income, in visibility, in prestige—all from book publishing.

You may have the raw data for a successful book in your files right now—without even knowing it!

Yet despite all this, many associations with a potentially successful book never get it into print. Or, if they do, most copies end up stacked in a storeroom—unsold and unread.

Why? Because of *a lack of knowledge of the publishing business*. Where do you begin? What's a realistic budget? How many copies do you print? The *Book Publishing for Associations* seminar will answer all these questions—and many more.

FREE
to seminar participants:
A $30 value

The Handbook of
Association Book Publishing
by Hubert Bermont

All participants in the seminar will receive—as a free bonus—a copy of *The Handbook of Association Book Publishing*, by Hubert Bermont.

This authoritative manual, just published, is *the first and only text on the subject of association book publishing*.

Following the structure of the seminar, it is divided into two parts: The Association as Author and The Association as Publisher. Packed with useful, practical information and advice, it covers everything from writing and editing to printing and distribution, and is fully indexed. Long after the seminar is over, you'll find yourself referring again and again to this indispensable volume—to answer questions, check facts, avoid problems, confirm decisions.

Casebound (in hard covers), the *Handbook* has an interior ring binding that opens flat for ease of reference. The cover is deep brown with gold stamping, and the text is printed on heavy, off-white stock. Handsomely designed and printed, it will make an impressive addition to your desk or shelf.

Priced at $30, *The Handbook of Association Book Publishing* is *free* to participants in the *Book Publishing for Associations* seminar.

NOTE: If you cannot attend the seminar, but wish to order a copy of *The Handbook of Association Book Publishing*, simply check the appropriate box on the attached form.

What you'll learn.

Here is the seminar agenda, along with highlights of the presentations:

The first day: The Association as Author
Why an association book? . . . Should you publish on your own—or seek an outside publisher? . . . Early mistakes—and how to avoid them. . . . How to choose the right title. . . . Writing and editing. . . . How to find a publisher. . . . How to submit for publication. . . . Negotiating with publishers: editorial decisions, contracts, money. . . . And more.

The second day: The Association as Publisher
When to become your own publisher. . . . How non-profit status affects publishing ventures. . . . Contracting with an author. . . . Copyright. . . . Designing the book. . . . A quick course in book production: typesetting, proofreading, pasteup, printing, binding. . . . Deciding on the number to print. . . . Pricing. . . . Marketing the book: public relations, direct mail, advertising, book clubs, selling at conferences and exhibitions. . . . Distribution and order fulfillment. . . . And more.

Who is Hubert Bermont?

No one else is better qualified than Hubert Bermont to lead a seminar on book publishing for association executives.

Head of his own publishing firm, executive director of Brentano's branch stores for 10 years, he is the author of 11 books, including *Getting Published* and *The Handbook of Association Book Publishing*.

As the world's first and only book consultant, Mr. Bermont lists among his clients the country's top publishing firms and national associations. He has been instrumental in the publication of more than 75 association books. Here are some of them:

- For the Chamber of Commerce of the United States, he negotiated the publication of *Pioneers of American Business* (Grosset and Dunlap).
- For the American Film Institute, he negotiated a multi-book contract with Little, Brown and served as liaison for the publication of the multi-volume *Catalog of American Film* (Bowker).
- For the Electronic Industries Association, he published *The Directory of Electronic Products and Services*.
- For the Air Force Association, he was responsible for the publication of *The Safe Driving Handbook* (Grosset and Dunlap). Several hundred thousand copies were sold.
- For the National Recreation and Parks Association, he negotiated the publication of *The Animals Next Door* (Fleet Press) and wrote and arranged for the publication of *New Approaches to Financing Parks and Recreation* (Acropolis).
- For the Smithsonian Institution, he negotiated distribution agreements with Random House and with the British publishing firm of David and Charles, Ltd.

Among Hubert Bermont's other clients are the American Association of Retired Persons, the American Association of University Women, the American Society of Association Executives, the American Booksellers Association, the National Education Association, the Retired Officers Association, the American Forest Institute, the National Academy of Sciences, the International Association of Chiefs of Police, the National Wildlife Federation, the American Federation of Teachers, the Brookings Institution, the International Reading Association and the National Retired Teachers Association.

A practical "hands-on" workshop.

Book Publishing for Associations is not simply a series of lectures, but a practical, *working* seminar.

You will be encouraged to bring along your own book project—whether it's just a rough concept or a completed manuscript. Mr. Bermont and the other seminar leaders will give you *personal advice and guidance* on whether the concept is viable, the best course to follow, how to cut your expenses, titling and pricing, which publishers to approach, and much more.

In addition, you may ask Mr. Bermont—and the other seminar leaders—any and all questions on your mind. Question-and-answer sessions and informal discussion periods will be frequent during both days of the seminar.

As a book consultant, Hubert Bermont charges his clients $40 an hour. *But seminar participants will be able to consult with him personally at no additional charge.*

The details.

Book Publishing for Associations will be held at the — —, Washington, D.C. on Monday and Tuesday, October 16 and 17, from 9 a.m. to 5 p.m.

If you register in advance, the seminar fee is $225. Additional persons from the same organization may attend for $200 each.

The seminar fee is completely inclusive—there are no additional charges of any kind. Here is what it covers:

- The entire two days of lectures, presentations and discussions.
- The "hands-on" workshop, analyzing participants' book projects.
- Free personal consultation with Mr. Bermont and the other seminar leaders.
- *The Handbook of Association Book Publishing*, by Hubert Bermont—a $30 value. (See box.)
- Lunch, coffee breaks and refreshment breaks.

Book Publishing for Associations is essential for professional and trade association executive directors, public relations directors and publications directors. And for anyone else concerned in any way with association book publishing.

You'll leave the seminar with a working knowledge of book publishing today, and with the skills to make sound decisions on every phase of your own book publishing projects.

To Register

Use the attached Advance Registration Form.
Please note that you'll save money if you register in advance.
Attendance is strictly limited, **so we urge you to**
mail your registration today.

ADVANCE REGISTRATION FORM
Bermont Books
815 15th St., N.W.
Washington, D.C. 20005

YES! Please register me for the *Book Publishing for Associations* seminar at the — — in Washington on October 16 and 17.

Name _____

Title _____

Organization _____

Address _____

City _____ State_____ Zip _____

Phone ( ) _____

☐ The following colleagues will be attending with me:

Name _____ Title _____

Name _____ Title _____

Name _____ Title _____

ADVANCE REGISTRATION FEES: $225 per person. Each additional person from your organization: $200.

☐ Enclosed is our check for a total of $ _____
☐ Please bill us.

I understand that the registration fee covers the full two-day seminar, workshop, personal consulting, lunch, refreshment breaks and all seminar materials, including *The Handbook of Association Book Publishing*.

☐ I can't attend the seminar, but would like to order a copy of *The Handbook of Association Book Publishing*.

☐ Enclosed is a check for $30.
☐ Bill us.

The seminar at a glance.

What's it all about? *Book Publishing for Associations* is a two-day seminar that teaches association executives the basics of book publishing. You'll leave with the knowledge and skills to handle your first book publishing project competently and successfully.

Who should attend? Association executive directors, public relations directors and directors of publications.

When? Monday and Tuesday, October 16 and 17, 1978. 9 a.m. to 5 p.m.

Where? — —, Washington, D.C.

How much? Advance registration fees (by Oct. 1): $225 per person; $200 for each additional person from the same organization. Registration after Oct. 1: $245 per person; $220 for each additional person from the same organization. A full refund will be granted for cancellations received *prior* to Oct. 10, 1978. No refunds will be granted for cancellations received *after* Oct. 10.

Confirmation? All registrations received by October 6 will be confirmed by mail.

How do I register? Use the convenient Advance Registration Form at right.

Hotel rooms? Accommodations are not included in the seminar fee. However, the — — will hold a block of rooms for seminar participants. Confirmation of your registration will include full information on rooms and rates. Please make reservations early directly with the hotel.

Questions? Call or write Hubert Bermont, Bermont Books, 815 Fifteenth St. N.W., Washington, D.C. 20005. (202) 737-6437.

ATTENDANCE IS LIMITED!
PLEASE REGISTER EARLY.

7. The Results

AS SEMINARS GO, I had a financial minor success. However, for a first endeavor, it was a major success. Here are the figures:

Expenses

Copywriter	$	650
Artwork		850
Mailing Lists		680
Printing		1200
Postage		1344
Mailing		255
Hotel & Refreshments		500
Study Materials		200
Total	$	5679

Income

35 Attendees @ $225	$	7875
85 books (gross profit)		2125
Total		$10,000.
NET PROFIT	$	4321

I write of the dubiousness of the success of this venture because $2,000 (not counting the book sales) is not a very good return for the kind of work and planning that went into this; it took a lot of effort and time—not to mention the risk. On the other side of the coin, I did pick up a goodly amount of consulting work as a result of this exposure. Here again, no matter how much knowledge a consultant imparts, the client will usually engage him with "So much for that; now how about *my* project?" Most important, I learned a lot of lessons about seminars. So one of the big pay-offs for my investment is my ability to pass those lessons along to you here in this book. Phone calls to prospective attendees proved the following:

1. The price was too low. My original assessment of about $300 would have been both more accurate and more fruitful. Price seemed to be no object because of the uniqueness of the seminar; it was *never* offered as an excuse for not attending.

2. The more important the executive (the higher up in the table of organization), the less he could afford to spend two full days at a seminar. He would have gladly paid the full fee for one day which would pack in all of the information—if that were possible.

3. I chose the wrong month. October turned out to be the heaviest administrative month for association executives, and they couldn't get away from their own internal meetings. (This was simply a case of sloppy research on my part.)

Here are statistics which bore a lot more information:

1. Thirty-five people attended the seminar.
2. Eighty-five others ordered the Handbook.
3. Sixty-five percent of the attendees were women. (I don't know why this surprised me, but it did.)
4. Seventy-five percent of the attendees came from out of town. Four came from Canada.

I concluded from this the following:

a) For a two-day seminar, the executive employee wants to be able to take an all-expenses-paid trip out of town. (This, of course, would not apply to the self-employed individual.) Since Washington, D.C. houses most of the nation's association executives and so few took advantage of a short *walk* from their offices to the motel, this conclusion was obvious.

b) My "insurance policy" in the form of the Handbook not only paid off, but prevented the project from being marginal.

The seminar went off beautifully. We asked the attendees to fill out commentary cards before leaving. Their reactions and impressions were gratifying, to say the least. They also gave me the impetus to continue with the program.

I made one additional error, which I'd like to tell you about. Most people who receive mail announcing a forthcoming relevant and interesting seminar usually discard it with the thought: "They'll contact me at least two more times before the event, so I'll throw this flyer away and make my decision when I hear from them again." I know that I ofttimes react this way. Since my budget only allowed for one mailing, I should have boldly indicated "THIS IS THE ONLY NOTICE YOU WILL RECEIVE." It would have prevented their careless discarding of my mailer and would have further enhanced the prestige of the seminar because the implication would be that the seminar is so successful we really don't need them.

8. Forecast

JUST BEFORE MY first seminar was scheduled to take place, I rented a tape recorder. It ran for the entire two days. Thereafter, I edited it down to four one-hour cassettes. To make duplicates from the master costs me $1 per cassette (or $4 per set). I shall offer these for sale in my next seminar announcement (along with the book) for $60 per set. Another source of income from the same promotion. In this instance, the objection I had before about cassettes is not valid because every association has a cassette player and I don't have to attempt to sell the equipment. If, on the other hand, your seminar is to individuals you will have to offer the player, too.

Ten people who could not attend the first seminar asked to be signed up for the next one. Their names and addresses were duly noted.

The first seminar, of course, engendered a certain amount of publicity in the form of news stories. This helped spread the word further.

Armed with all of this and my testimonials from the first seminar, it is far from "pollyannish" to be sanguine about the second one. Undoubtedly the attendance will be somewhat greater as will the sale of the Handbooks. Add to that whatever additional sales I get from the cassettes, and I should realize a handsome profit. But let's be ultra-conservative about this and just figure that the return will be no more than the first. The figures stack up this way: (Note that the copywriter and artist fees have been eliminated and the printing fee drops due to the negatives being re-used and only slightly altered.)

Expenses

Mailing Lists	$ 680
Printing	1025
Postage	1344
Mailing	255
Hotel & Refreshments	500
Study Materials	200
Personal travel, food and hotel out of town	200
Total	$ 4204

Income

35 Attendees @ $285	$ 9975
85 books (gross profit)	2125
Total	$12,100
NET PROFIT	$ 7895

I intend to hold these seminars twice a year (May and November) and add minimally $16,000 to my regular income. Undoubtedly this figure will be much higher due to natural growth and the sale of cassettes, but I am being as conservative as possible throughout this book in the area of projections.

To accommodate the "out-of-town" syndrome, I have decided to hold the seminar in a city somewhere near the three major association repositories, i.e. Washington, New York and Chicago—probably Boston. Let me explain. If I were to hold the next one in Chicago, for example, the Chicagoans probably wouldn't come. I have also ruled out a resort because the attendees would feel torn between the sessions and the golf-links.

I feel now that I have all of my "ducks in a row" concerning my seminars. I no longer feel that it is a risk. I wish I'd had someone to tell me these things before I tried my first one and "sweated it out". I feel good about being able to pass my experiences (the good and the bad) along to you.

- **Afterword**
- **Index**
- **Appendix**

Afterword

The combined activities of authoring, publishing and lecturing in my consultative field now produce more income than does my consulting practice. I freely confess, however, that they are not quite as personally rewarding or gratifying as the one-on-one work I do with my clients. Fortunately, I don't have to make a choice, since I am able to divide my time without strain. Should I ever be faced with alternatives, I would always regard my consultancy as inviolate, because that is what I enjoy the most.

Having gone over this manuscript in detail, I am satisfied that I have shared with you everything I know, experienced and learned in these three areas of endeavor. I do hope that I have "lit your candle" and that you will prosper and enjoy yourself at least as much as I have—and even more.

> Hubert Bermont
> Washington, D.C.
> January 1979

Index

A

Accreditation, 21
Advance, 25, 27, 30, 33, 77
Advertising, 25, 26, 34, 55,
    57, 58, 61-69, 75, 76, 85
American Forest Institute, 34
Audio/visuals, 90, 93, 94
Author's alterations, 31

B

Bernstein, Leonard, 65
Binding, 47, 48, 51, 52, 55,
    57, 76
Blue-lines, 51
Body Building, 78
Book club, 68
Book manufacturer, 48
Bookstores, 55, 57, 58, 61
Book writing, 17-19
Bowker & Co., 22, 46
Brentano's, 61
Business Week, 75
Buying Country Property, 34

C

Cassettes, 77, 90, 109, 110
Catalogue, 58
Changes, 51
Chapters, 17
Checks, 72
Christian Science Monitor, 75
Coding, 62-64
Combined Book Exhibit, 68
Complimentary copies, 75, 76
Comprehensiveness, 19, 21
Consignment, 61
Contracts, 23, 25, 29-31
Conventions, 68
Copy-editing, 31
Copyright, 22, 26, 30, 45, 46
Copywriter, 63, 65, 76, 97,
    98, 105, 109
Coupon, 62, 63, 65, 75
Credibility, 21

D

Design, 26, 41-43, 47, 48,
    51, 53, 54, 76

Direct mail, 61-63, 67, 78, 89,
    97-104
Discounts, 68, 69, 88

E

Editors, 22, 26, 27
Encyclopedia Britannica, 48
Estimates, 47, 48

F

Fleet Press, 33
Foreign rights, 68
Free Enterprise, 75
Fulfillment, 62, 64, 71-73

G

Galleys, 31, 49, 50
Getting Published, 12, 15, 33,
    34, 77
Guarantee, 43, 58, 67

H

*Handbook Of Association
    Book Publishing*, 85, 107
Harper & Row, 33, 47
Honoraria, 15
Hotels, 89, 90, 105, 110
How To Avoid Probate, 34
*How To Become A Successful
    Consultant In Your Own
    Field*, 39, 43, 75, 76, 78

I

Imprint, 39, 40, 72
Index, 17, 19, 31, 32, 51
Introduction, 17
Invoicing, 57, 71
Inventory, 30, 46, 77
ISBN, 45, 46

J

Jiffy bag, 71, 76

K

Keying (see coding)

L

Label, 62, 71, 72
Lasser's Tax Guide, 34
Libraries, 68, 69
Library of Congress, 45
List broker, 62
List manager, 78
List rental, 78
Literary Marketplace, 22

M

Magazine, 62, 63, 67, 85
Magazine article, 15-17
Mailing lists, 62, 105, 110
Mailing piece, 62, 97-104, 107
Market survey, 54, 58
Marketing, 26, 30, 39, 53, 55,
    57, 58, 61-69, 85

McGraw-Hill, 47
Mechanicals, 47, 48, 51, 52, 57
Memoirs of Richard Nixon, 48
Money, 78
Multiple submissions, 22, 23

N

National Recreation & Park
   Association, 34
National Review, 75
Negatives, 30, 54
Negotiation, 25-27
*New Approaches To Financing
   Parks and Recreation*, 34
Newsletter, 62, 63, 75, 78, 79, 85
Newsletter Yearbook Directory, 63
Newspapers, 63, 67, 75
Non-delivery, 72, 73

O

Out of print, 26, 30
Overhead, 57, 58

P

Packing, 64, 71
Page proofs, 31, 51
Pagination, 23, 31, 51
Paste-ups (see mechanicals)
People, 78
P.I., 63, 64, 75, 76

Postage, 64, 67, 71-73, 76, 105
Preferred space, 67
Prentice-Hall, 47
Press release, 67, 75
Pricing, 26, 27, 30, 42, 53, 57-59, 62, 67, 68, 85, 87, 105, 110
Printing, 41, 47-49, 51-55, 57, 76, 105, 109, 110
Production, 25, 42, 47-52, 55, 57, 58
Proofing, 31, 32, 49-51
Public speaking, 83
Publishers, 21-34, 47, 55, 57-59, 62

R

Random House, 47
Refunds, 64, 67
Register of Copyrights, 45
Rejections, 23
Reprint, 49, 54, 55, 75, 76
Reproofing, 50
Residuals, 26
Retirement, 75
Returns, 57, 58, 64, 67, 76
Reviews, 63, 67, 69
Revised edition, 26
Risk, 54, 55, 58, 62-64, 105, 110
Robotyping, 63
Royalties, 12, 25, 29, 30, 33, 57, 58, 77, 78
Running heads, 51

S

Sales commissions, 57, 58
Seminars, 68, 69, 83-110
Shipping, 64
Signatures, 51
Split edition, 67
Standard Rate & Data, 63
Subject Guide To Books In Print, 22
Subsidiary rights, 26, 29, 33
Symbols, 50

T

Table of Contents, 19
Tape recorder, 109
Tests, 62, 67
Time, 65
Titles, 17-19, 26, 39
Trade fairs, 68
Translation rights, 68
TX, 45
Typesetting, 47-51, 53, 54, 57

U

U.S. Postal Service, 71

V

Valley Of The Dolls, 48
Van Dykes (see blue-lines)
Vanity publishing, 15, 22, 40

W

Wall Street Journal, 67, 75
Warehousing, 57, 73
What A Waste, 34
Workshop, 87, 97

X

Xeroxing, 19, 23, 51

Appendix

Partial List of the Author's Clients

Acropolis Books, Ltd.
A.F. of L. - C.I.O.
Air Force Association
American Association of Retired Persons
American Association of University Women
American Booksellers Association
American Federation of Teachers
American Film Institute
American Forest Institute
Ballantine Books
BFS Psychological Associates
B'nai B'rith
R.R. Bowker Company
The Brookings Institution
Catholic University
Chamber of Commerce of the United States
Data Solutions
Electronic Industries Association
Evelyn Wood Reading Dynamics
The Washington Star
Federation of American Societies for Experimental Biology
Garfinckels

Goodway
Grosset & Dunlap
Harper & Row
Human Events
International Reading Association
Journal of the Armed Forces
McGrath Publishing Company
McGraw-Hill
Metromedia
National Academy of Sciences
National Education Association
National Portrait Gallery
National Recreation & Park Association
National Wildlife Federation
Nation's Business
Optimum Book Marketing Company
Pitman Publishing Company
Random House
The New Republic
Retired Officers Association
The Smithsonian Institution
Stein & Day
United States Department of the Interior
The Viking Press
WETA-TV
James T. White & Company

This book has been set Times Roman, twelve point type with two points additional leading and printed on 80 pound paper.

Typesetting by: Patricia C. Haxton
Printing by: Corporate Press